Kern County: The Path to Secession and a New Constitution

By Don Durrett

September 2014

ISBN: 978-1-4276-5518-9

BOOKS BY DON DURRETT

A Stranger From the Past

Conversations With an Immortal

Finding Your Soul

New Thinking for the New Age

Spirit Club

Finding Your Soul Workbook

Last of the Gnostics

The Gathering

How to Invest in Gold & Silver: A Complete Guide with a Focus on Mining Stocks

The Demise of America: The Coming Breakup of The United States and What Will Replace It

Edited by Kiera Coffee

I place economy among the first and most important virtues, and public debt as the greatest of dangers to be feared. To preserve our independence, we must not let our rulers load us with perpetual debt.

– Thomas Jefferson

Beware the greedy hand of government thrusting itself into every corner and crevice of industry.

– Thomas Paine

When the people find that they can vote themselves money, that will herald the end of the republic.

– Benjamin Franklin

For Jane Watts, my English 1A and 1B
teacher at Bakersfield College, who
inspired me to be a writer.

CONTENTS

Introduction xi

Preface.. xvii

Chapter One: It Begins 1

Chapter Two: The Committee 75

Chapter Three: The Interviews 91

Chapter Four: Door to Door 109

Chapter Five: Time to Prepare 131

Chapter Six: The Vote 147

Chapter Seven: Civil Disobedience 167

Chapter Eight: Isabella is Born........................ 181

Afterword.. 205

Appendix: New Constitution 221

INTRODUCTION

This book is written with the assumption that America is on the verge of an economic crisis. A crisis so severe that it will lead to a secession movement within our borders. If that assumption turns out to be false, then this will be a work of hyperbole and perhaps a good "what-if" book. But if it's right, then this book has important concepts about reorganizing the country that may need to be considered.

I have believed since the early 1990s that Texas would secede first, and form The Republic of Texas. That belief has become stronger as our economic system approaches bankruptcy. Texas is ripe for secession for a number of reasons. The most important being that it existed as an independent country from 1836 to 1846. Other reasons include: Texans are extremely independent; they love being Texans; they love their flag, which you see waving everywhere in the state; they do not like Washington D.C.; they have an immigration problem that Washington is ignoring; they are the only state with their own electrical grid; and they have an abundance of oil, which they can monetize.

The secession movement that I envisioned as early as 1991 is now alive and well. In 2014, Crimea voted to secede from Ukraine; Venice voted to secede from Italy; Scotland voted for independence; and Catalonia in Spain is close to voting. More than a dozen additional secession movements exist throughout the world. In the U.S., there are secession movements in Texas, Colorado, California, and Maryland.

This book is based on the premise that Texas will secede after an economic crisis, which will lead to a series of victorious secessions movements throughout the country. After Texas secedes, the entire country will break up into regional countries resulting in a very weak national government like the European Union. Not only do states become new countries, but so do some counties.

I chose Kern County and Bakersfield as my model location, because it is both my hometown and it has many of the vital requirements for a victorious secession movement. This area is a prime agricultural area, and has large oil production. These two industries practically make it crash-proof. All it will need in the future is good leadership in order to easily thrive. Also, it is not a highly populated area, making it ideal for avoiding riots and chaos. And because it is an agricultural and oil producing community, the majority of the citizens are hard working people. This isn't a retirement community. There is a very strong work ethic in this county, with a lot of blue collar workers. This is a conservative patriotic community, that would never think of seceding today, or seceding first. But it is also pragmatic, and may seize an opportunity if it arises. If secession is the only way to rebuild the community, I feel Kern County will likely choose it.

I use a story to show what could happen. While the odds of this story coming true are infinitesimally small, parts of it could become the future in some manner. Once I got the idea to write a story about secession, I felt compelled to begin immediately, and the draft was written in only two months. Society is clearly strained and in dire need of change, and it is becoming apparent that the type of change needed will not be forthcoming from the government.

Once I had the idea to write about secession I knew I had to write a new constitution. That seemed the only way to fix our problems. I've been a harsh critic of our current system (political, economic, social) and want something better. Let's face it, society has its share of entrenched problems that need to be fixed. We have created a place where the majority or people are living with a lack of contentment. It's time for a better way to live. It's time to start over.

Our problems have progressed to the point where I am tired of people referring to America as the greatest country on Earth. I think that used to be true, but no more. We can no longer claim to be number one, without other countries smirking at our hubris. They know we have fallen, and so should we. If we are such a great country, then I don't think the secession movement would be progressing. And I don't think that our problems would have become so intractable.

It's ironic that I'm going to write about solutions, because I don't believe there are any solutions to our current problems — unless we start over. Secession and a new constitution allow for a complete reorganization of a community or a country. Reorganization makes change possible. One of my previous books, titled, *The Demise of America*, conveys the premise that America is doomed to economic collapse and reorganization. That premise carries to this book, although this time I offer solutions.

The secession movement today is about reorganizing society. The biggest reason for these movements is that citizens are tired of being controlled by an ineffective large government. The fictional storyline of this book is different from actual secession movements. The secession of Kern County shows what happens after the fall of the U.S. Economy, and after the breakup of the U.S. I'm not talking about stumble, but a full-fledged fall, where we are bankrupt and we do not recover.

Under this scenario, the U.S. becomes divided into a series of countries. The national government becomes very weak and has little impact on the affairs of the countries. Each of these new countries will write new constitutions. Kern County could possibly follow the path that I layout in this book, but it is only a model and vision of one possibility. It is inevitable in my opinion that this fall of the U.S. is coming, and reorganizing with new constitutions is likely something that will unfold.

It's 2014 and much of what I'm going to write about in this book will be outdated very shortly. However, the current state of the U.S. economic situation is the reason for the book. I need to write about it even if it will soon be history. Most likely you will read this book a few years down the road, after secession becomes a hot topic.

The U.S. Economy is heading for a collapse that will change our way of life. It's unavoidable in my opinion and puts us on a collision course with secession and the breakup of the country. It's that transparent to me. This is why I think Texas is destined to secede. If Texas is still a state by 2020, I'll be very surprised. Change is coming soon and it will likely pick up speed once it begins. If I had to give a date for Texas secession, then I would bet on 2018, which is not that far away.

* * * * *

This book will be controversial for many reasons. Some people will not like me popularizing or advocating secession. Others will not like me portraying civil disobedience. I did not want to glamorize civil disobedience, but I thought it was unlikely that a new country in the middle of California could be formed in a completely innocuous manner. There are a lot of interest groups that will be impacted if the constitution I propose is approved. The list is quite long: corporations, corporate employees, government employees, pensioners, veterans, the disabled, schools, healthcare workers, financial industries. The change that is suggested is quite revolutionary. Perhaps the vision is too broad, but I think that is the only solution.

I also want to state for the record that I wrote this new constitution without any notes in about two days. All of the ideas in the constitution are my own (except the preamble, which I borrowed from Thomas Jefferson). I write this down because I know that in the future there are going to be many constitutions written, and I think I might be the first. I wrote this new constitution hoping to fix all of our problems and create a community that is prosperous, harmonious, ethical, joyful, humane, and a wonderful place to live. I think I got it right, but we'll probably never know.

Don Durrett

4/24/2014

PREFACE

It happened fast, much faster than anyone expected. One late Friday afternoon, an AP news release stated that Saudi Arabia was no longer going to accept U.S. dollars for their oil exports. By Monday morning the global stock markets were in a tailspin. The U.S. stock market opened down 5% and finished the day down 8% from a bombardment of selling. The days that followed only seemed to get worse. Within two weeks, the global stock markets were all down more than 15% or more, and the U.S. stock markets were down 25%.

The television financial news pundits tried to calm fears by postulating that the pull-back was not unusual after a long multi-year rally. Politicians and the President tried to extoll the virtues of a so-called recovery, but the dominos continued to fall. The drop in the stock markets decreased liquidity as banks hunkered down and stopped making loans. This left many companies scrambling to rollover debt in order to remain solvent. It was the crash of 2008 all over again, and several major financial institutions were on the verge of bankruptcy.

A major New York bank had to be bailed out, then two major insurance companies. The Federal Reserve Bank printed the money and gave it to them. We were in crisis mode again. One corporation after another started announcing layoffs to protect their stock share price, including their CEO's job. Then the second shoe dropped; China started selling their U.S. Treasury bonds, they were running for the sidelines, hoping to sell before the economy crashed. They recognized that the U.S. wasn't going to be able to survive this crisis. After they sold $250 billion bonds in one week, the Japanese were forced to sell some of their U.S. Treasury bonds. They couldn't sit on the sidelines and allow

China to sell all of their bonds. No one wanted to be left holding the bag of worthless debt.

As predicted by many analysts, once the bond selling began, interest rates rose. The U.S. Government was furious with the Chinese for starting this panic, but what could the U.S. do? Start a war over something that we did to ourselves? The Chinese were looking at the long term and recognized that we had likely destroyed our economy. They were going to take us down economically and then focus on the rest of the world for their trading partners.

Once interest rates rose, the derivatives market blew up. A financial derivative is a fancy term for financial insurance. However, the $700 trillion derivatives market had always been a charade, because the holders of the derivatives were insuring each other. If one major financial company failed, they all failed. The Federal Reserve Bank had to choose between bailing out a group of large financial institutions, or buying all of China's and Japan's U.S. Treasury bonds. This much money printing would surely cause hyper-inflation. They were trapped and the U.S. Government had no choice but to default on their national debt.

After the default, U.S. Government spending was cut dramatically, because no more debt could be raised. Without EBT (Electronic Benefit Transfer) cards to pay for food, riots erupted throughout the country. Most of the large cities had to declare martial law. After nine months of rioting and economic malaise, Texas seceded and formed The Republic of Texas. The secession movement in the U.S. had officially begun.

The default caused the U.S. Dollar to devalue and it continued to drop. This created an increase in prices for food and other necessities, while at the same time there were massive layoffs in healthcare, finance, government jobs, consumer retail, and the services sector. Small businesses were closing in waves. It didn't appear that any help was on the way. The citizens believed it was going to get worse before it got better.

Within three years the United States no longer existed. It had broken up in to a series of countries. All that was left of the United States government was a feckless group of bureaucrats who tried to help the new countries develop inter-country commerce and trade laws.

CHAPTER ONE: IT BEGINS

John was forty-three. Six feet tall and handsome with a calm disposition. He was well-read in a variety of subjects with an MBA. He could have been a college professor, but had no interest in joining the establishment. His hobbies were writing metaphysical books and public lecturing. He was a deep thinker and a spiritual man, a philosopher. His wife Julie provided grounding to their life. She was an artist and was much more practical. They did not have any children. They tried to conceive when they were first married, but were unsuccessful. They decided that children were not necessary for their happiness did not pursue fertility doctors.

For fun they liked to watch movies together and travel. Without kids around, they tended to travel a lot. A four day weekend to Hawaii was not unusual for them. They were deeply in love and enjoyed each other's company. Both of them were social people and liked to hang out with friends from time to time. However, because of their comfort level with each other, they tended to spend most of their time together.

John had recently lost his job as computer systems analyst and now spent most of his time reading online news and various postings by other Internet users. That day he read a news item on Zerohedge that Humboldt County was planning a referendum to secede from California. They wanted to form their own country and grow marijuana. After all, Northern California was perhaps the best place in the world to grow pot. John had read of other county secession movements, and clearly it had come to California. He had an epiphany. Why not his own Kern County?

It had a low population of less than 1 million people over 8,000 square miles. The only city of any size was Bakersfield at

350,000 people. The only other city of any size was Delano, which was relatively small at 55,000 people. The other nine cities in the county were all small. Thus, they had plenty of space for everyone and didn't have a crowding problem.

The assets of Bakersfield and Kern County were substantial. There were vast acres of high quality farmland. Thus, they could easily feed themselves and export the rest. Next, they had oil. Kern County was the largest oil producing county in the country, with over a billion barrels of reserves. Between oil production and agriculture, the county was practically crash-proof, and provided a foundation to the local economy.

The oil and agriculture related industries required substantial financial services from the large flow of income they provided. This made Bakersfield's banking and insurance industries fairly strong and stable. It is not an understatement to say there was a lot of money in Bakersfield, and if you drove around you would see a lot of affluent areas.

There was a local university, but most of the locals were educated at colleges in other cities and returned to live here. It could be said that the local population was well educated and there was a strong sense of business acumen.

So, Bakersfield wasn't a backwater city. They could hold their own with any city in America. Bill Thomas represented Kern County and was chairman of the House Ways and Means Committee during the George W. Bush administration. Kevin McCarthy was the House Majority Leader during the Obama administration. Both of these politicians were well respected conservative Republicans. Bakersfield is considered one of the most conservative cities not only in California, but the entire nation, although that had been slowly changing because of demographics.

These changes included a recent influx of immigration from Mexico. In 1970, Bakersfield was about 70% Caucasian, but today that figure is below 50%. This influx has impacted the community in significant ways. Many first and second generation Hispanic Americans have found it difficult to thrive economically. The result of which has led to more gang affiliations and lower class neighborhoods. Moreover, the education system in the Bakersfield City School District has had poorer results in recent years, with the same bifurcation witnessed throughout the country, with many affluent families leaving for the Panama School District in the suburbs.

John knew from growing up in Bakersfield that it was changing dramatically. No longer was Bakersfield going to be a conservative white community. Now there were two major diverse groups (Democratic Hispanics and Republican whites) that had to find a way to get along.

John thought to himself, we have agriculture, oil, and water. Plus, we don't have a large population. We have a big advantage over most of the country. We could easily go it alone and finance ourselves.

He decided to build a web page called *Kern County: The Road to Secession*. He would blog every day and begin his own movement. He didn't see any other hope for the economy. From his perspective it was only going to get worse. It was time to go it alone and find the answers to problems locally. California was broke. They either changed or withered away. It was time for proactive change, and not the kind of change that politicians were always promising.

Using a website template, he had the website up and running in only a few days. On the main page he posted his reason for secession,[1] along with his proposed constitution.[2] He created an

---

1   Refer to Afterword at the end of the book.
2   Refer to Appendix.

excellent forum where anyone who joined for free could make their own posts, and anyone could reply to a post as a guest.

It didn't take long before the forum became a busy place, with 1,000+ comments every day. At first, nearly all of the comments came from outside of Kern County, but over time more and more people from the local area began to post.

John decided to create a Facebook page and a Bakersfield Meetup group. One of the poster's on his website offered a large meeting room where they could discuss the new constitution.

The Meetup group list had 500 people after only two weeks. The first meeting was scheduled for the first Saturday of the month at 1 p.m. John purchased a low cost public address system for the large room. The display screen showed the title of the presentation: *A New Constitution.*

"Good afternoon, and thank you for coming." He opened.

Many in the audience stood and began clapping. John was taken aback and did not expect such a response. He smiled and bowed. He looked at the crowd and recognized a few friends, which gave him inspiration.

"Thanks for the reception. It appears there are a lot of like-minded people in the audience. We have recognized that the U.S. economic and political model has failed, or is in the process of failing. It's time for a new beginning.

"I'm going to present my proposal for a new constitution. I want you to keep an open mind and recognize that this proposal is only for Kern Country. It is not a system that necessarily will work for a larger area or larger population."

John paused. He was wondering if the audience would be receptive to his new constitution. He got the impression that the audience was listening intently, which gave him confidence to continue.

"Today I would like to have a discussion about the Articles and the Bill of Rights, although I will read the Declaration, Guiding Principles, Overall Philosophy, and Businesses Philosophy. We will talk about these at our next meeting. With our limited time today, I would like to try to cover all of the Articles. If we have enough time, then we will also do the Bill of Rights.

"Okay, let's begin." He pressed the remote and the first slide appeared.

Declaration

> We the people of Isabella desire to form an independent country that provides its people a community based on fairness, freedom, integrity, honor, justice, equality, and respect. The community will exist as a united whole that works together in harmony with cooperation. No one person or one group shall infringe upon the rights of others. Government shall remain limited in scope and size, with the citizens in charge of making all important decisions.

"Oh yeah, by the way, our new country is going be called Isabella. I thought of calling it Bakersfield or Kern, but Isabella is a beautiful name. And our beautiful Lake Isabella can be leveraged into a country name. I'm open to suggestions if someone has a better name, but it's pretty good."

John read the slide, then pressed the remote.

Guiding Principles

1. Liberty to be free without encumbrance.

2. Every human a respected sovereign being with equal basic human rights.

3. Opportunity for everyone, and no one deprived of education and basic necessities.

4. Service to the community and not service to ones self.

5. If a person cries out for help, the community will come to their aid.

6. Crime will not be tolerated.

7. Government kept to a minimal level.

8. Thrive and enjoy life.

9. Reach for your dreams, but you may have to work hard to achieve them.

10. Respect the environment, which includes earth, water, air, and all life forms.

After John read the slide, he pressed the remote.

Overriding Philosophy

We are all neighbors and should treat each other fairly and kindly. We are all equals and should consider the humanity of our actions. Helping one another should be a priority for everyone.

John looked at Julie who was standing nearby. She was wearing a blue mini dress and looked pretty with her long red hair. He smiled at her and then pressed the remote. Anyone paying attention, would have noticed that Julie was part of the lecture.

She had a serious demeanor and was watching both John and the crowd intently. Her formal dress and the strategic place where she stood was a clue to her importance. When John smiled at her, it was obvious she was involved in some way.

Business Philosophy

Our goal is sustainability over growth, stability over complexity, quality of life over achievement. While competition is required in a capitalistic system, conflict and battle do not have over shadow our humanity.

Article I

Section 1

The will be no elected officials or politicians. Government employees will serve 1-year terms appointed by decision review boards (DRBs). Citizens of Isabella will be obligated to serve once every 5 years. They can volunteer for jobs or be assigned. Medical exemptions will be available for the infirm.

John read the slide and then looked across the audience to measure their response. "This reading will take a few hours to get through. The purpose of this meeting is to get feedback and share ideas. However, if we spend too much time on each section we will never finish. Two people will be given the opportunity to ask questions on each section, and then we can have a question and answer session at the end of the presentation if there is time. There are two microphones that can be passed around for each question. Raise your hand and we will find you."

John and Julie had asked two of their friends. Tammy and Kelley to be volunteers to help with his presentation. They were in charge of handing out microphones.

Immediately ten people raised their hands. While the volunteers handed out the microphones, John had one final request. "Please stand to ask your question."

John pointed at someone standing with a microphone.

"John, first I want to thank you for taking the initiative of making this happen. My question is how much will we get paid for our one year of government service? And will our employers be able to fire us if we leave our place of work for a year?"

John replied, "Your second question is easy to answer. Once you've read the entire constitution, you will know that the foundation of the law is based on a concept called Disturbing the Harmony of the Community. Anyone who fires an employee for doing their duty to the community would clearly be in violation and sentenced by an arbitration panel of their peers

"Your first question is more complicated. The annual salaries for working for the government will be determined by the main DRB. I would expect that there will be different pay scales for different jobs. Perhaps we could have three or four different tiers. All of this can be decided by the DRB."

John pointed to the only other member of the audience who was standing.

"My question is about the first main DRB board. I understand from your website that the DRB will consist of five men and five women and they will replace themselves, but who appoints the first group?"

John paused. "I've thought about it, but I haven't written anything down yet. From my perspective we want the first group to be carefully selected because they are going to organize the government by selecting various DRBs and arbitration panels.

They will also set the first minimum wage and first government salaries. And they will have the authority to enact new laws. So this will be a very powerful group of people for our first year of existence.

"I think the first group should be selected using an election. Each candidate can write an essay explaining why they should be on the first DRB and post it on my website. In addition, they will be asked to include their biography. Then the public can post their responses to the essays. This information can be used for an online voting system to elect the first DRB."

John pressed the remote, and read the next slide.

Article I

Section 2

Decision review board members will serve 1-year terms and will appoint their replacements. A citizen can only serve on a DRB once every 5 years. Each DRB will consist of 10 members, with 7 members representing a quorum. The number of DRBs necessary for conducting government businesses can be determined by the main DRB. All secondary DRBs shall hold the same level of authority, with the main DRB as the final arbiter.

John pointed at the next questioner who was standing.

"There seems to be a lot of detail missing. For instance, how often will the DRB meet? What kind of laws can they create? Are there any checks and balances?"

"They will meet as often as they deem necessary," John replied. "Since they have to vote for all new laws in public and take direct questions from citizens, I would expect them to meet publicly quite often. They will be full-time government employees for one year and have a duty to uphold. They can create any law they deem necessary.

"As for checks and balances, that is the beauty of this constitution. No one has the opportunity to amass any power. The entire government is replaced every year. Any decisions that were deemed inappropriate can be overturned by the next main DRB or by the citizens. Overturning laws is in another section."

John pointed at the next questioner with a microphone.

"Why does the main DRB get to choose their successors? Won't they just choose their family or friends?"

"This method will create continuity and will ensure that the constitution is respected," John replied. "No one will appoint a successor they don't trust. I wanted to eliminate politicians and avoid political elections, but we can't eliminate elections completely. For, as you will find out, there must be a way to hear the voice of citizens to revoke bad laws. However, we can eliminate annual elections to select government officials. The DRB will want to ensure the continuity of society. I'm confident they will select the best people for the job. Also, each DRB member alone will have very little power. Without a majority vote, new laws cannot be passed. For this reason, it will be very difficult for a bad law to get passed."

John paused and pressed the remote control, then read the next section.

Article I

Section 3

There shall be no judges or juries. The main DRB will have the authority to assign or delegate to other DRBs, the task of creating

1-year arbitration panels for all disputes, crimes, and misdemeanors. There can be several DRBs and several arbitration panels... whatever the main DRB deems necessary.

John pointed to one of the standing questioners. He was beginning to feel confident that he had the crowd's support and that the evening was going to go smoothly. Julie had given him a pep talk before the lecture and gave him enough inspiration to read the constitution and answer that audience's questions. Her support made it that much easier. Knowing that she believed in it was a powerful catalyst.

The woman with the microphone said, "If I understand this correctly, government will consist of DRBs and arbitration panels. All of which will consist of five men and five women, and requiring seven people for a quorum. The DRBs and panels will consist of citizens who work for the government for one year, and are paid a salary based on what the main DRB decides."

John nodded.

"Okay, then does this mean the main DRB has the most authority and can tell the other DRBs and panels what to do? Can they fire people? Also, what about expenses, travel, and vacations? Who decides all of these details?"

John smiled. "Great questions. The answer is simple, yes, the main DRB can do all of these things. They are the leaders who get to decide what is in the best interest of the community. This one group is where the power resides and it is their responsibility to make the right decisions. They can decide all of the details you listed or they can delegate that authority to a secondary DRB."

John pointed for the next question.

"It seems to me that the arbitration panels are going to replace our court system. Is this wise? Do we really want to eliminate judges and juries?"

"I think so," John replied. "The problem with judges is they are biased. There is no such thing as an impartial judge. For this reason, we need to do something different if we are going to change our ways. Society has become corrupt, and the court system is part of that corruption. As long as the new arbitration panels are impartial, I think the system will work wonderfully."

John looked at a man in the front row who seemed to be skeptical. He decided to expound on the differences between the current justice system and his new proposed system.

"The new arbitration panels will be appointed in a non-political way. There will be no political parties and no organizations. Those who sit on arbitration panels or DRBs will do so as servers to the community. While not all arbitration panels will be completely impartial, you can appeal a decision twice. This is explained in Article I, Section 6. It is unlikely all three panels will be biased."

John looked at the skeptical man in the front row whose expression did not change. He wondered if had gotten through to him. He pressed the remote and read the next section.

Article I

Section 4

The main DRB has the authority to implement new laws, enter into trade agreements, and coin money. However, these laws and agreements can be re-written and changed by the succeeding DRBs. The citizens can vote to overturn these laws by a majority vote. There shall be no citizen voting to implement laws, only to overturn laws. Moreover, laws should be kept to a minimum (refer to Article II). All main DRB decisions will be made at public meetings.

John pointed to the next questioner.

"The DRB can implement any law? There are no restrictions? What kind of money will they coin? Will there be a treasury department to collect taxes and coin the money? And how can we keep laws to a minimum? How can that be enforced?"

John smiled. "Thank you for the questions. I have a helper here in the front. My wife Julie is writing down the questions in case I forget them. So if I look over at Julie, it's because I forgot the question.

"First of all, yes, the DRB can make any law. However, it is up to the citizens to maintain their constitution. If a law is passed that is contrary to the constitution, the citizens should overturn it. This process is in another article which we will get to.

"Our paper currency will be backed by gold and convertible into gold. It will literally be a gold based monetary system. We will create our own mint and mint our own gold and silver coins. The DRB will be in charge of determining the size of the money supply, but it can only grow at a certain rate annually. This is in another article which we will cover today.

"No, we will not have a treasury department. The mint will be a private company that is paid by the citizens. Taxes can also be collected by a private company. And they can be audited by yet another private company.

"Lastly about your question of how laws can be kept to a minimum? The answer is in the Constitution's guiding principles. However, there is no law or article that prohibits new laws. We can only have faith that the guiding principles are maintained.

Creating a statute that we can only have one new law per year makes no sense, because a single law can be a thousand pages or more in length."

John turned to Julie. "What did I miss?" He listened to her and then turned back to the audience and smiled. "I answered them all."

John pointed to the next questioner.

"How often will we have these citizen votes? Who is eligible to vote? And how will we vote?"

"That's the next section," John replied.

He pressed the remote and then read the next section.

Article I

Section 5

Voting will occur on the 1st Tuesday in November if during the year 10% of the populace signs a petition to overturn a law. Digital signatures and digital voting are both acceptable. All citizens 21 years of age or older are eligible.

John provided an explanation. "Voting will occur once a year, and any law can be subject to be overturned if ten percent of the citizens sign a petition. This doesn't state that an ID is required to vote, but it is implied. I would expect each vote to be validated against citizenship records to maintain one vote per citizen. Perhaps we could require a government ID card to vote, and then scan the ID when someone votes. The DRB can figure this out. I'm hoping to use a combination of computer based voting from our homes and voting booths, and perhaps a one-week voting period."

John pointed at the next questioner.

"Why is the voting age twenty-one? Why not eighteen?"

John grimaced. "I knew that question would come up. The reason why is two-fold. First, teenagers are mostly clueless when it comes to politics or what is good for a country. I know from experience that I didn't have a clue how the world worked when I was a teenager. If you asked me to explain the difference between a liberal and conservative, I couldn't have told you. The second reason is to instill a sense of privilege into young people. Having to wait until you are twenty-one to vote gives it an air of importance. When I was eighteen and went to vote for the first time, I didn't feel empowered. Instead I felt obligated. After all, I was still a teenager and I didn't want to be bothered. That first experience did not instill in me a privilege of being able to vote."

John pointed for the next questioner.

"Why can't citizens vote to create laws?"

John replied. "We don't want to create a political culture. If the citizens are in charge of creating laws, everyone is going to be clamoring for this and that. This is the opposite of our guiding principles. We want to keep government to a minimum. The only referendums that we will have are those that are deemed necessary. The DRBs can create the laws that we need, which should be minimal."

John pressed the remote for the next slide and read it.

Article I

Section 6

All arbitration decisions must be reached within 3 months of the filing. Decisions regarding disputes and crimes can be appealed twice. This can be considered a three strikes process. After three derogatory decisions, it is final. The appeals process must be completed within three years of the first arbitration decision. There is one exception to the three strikes process. If new evidence is discovered, it can be presented to a DRB, which can reinitiate a new arbitration case. If the evidence is compelling, there is no statue of limitations.

John looked at Julie who smiled back. He thought about how she should be sharing the stage with him because she was as excited about this new constitution as he was. Both of them had spent many hours discussing how society was decaying and what could be done to fix their problems. In many respects, she was just as passionate about the need for fixing our problems as John.

John pointed for the next questioner.

"How do you file a dispute? Are you allowed to hire lawyers to represent your claim?"

"For filing disputes," John began, "a private company will be used to handle claims. This company will work with the main DRB to create necessary arbitration panels. As you will see in another section, frivolous claims will not be tolerated. The police will use the same process. If they discover a citizen or visitor in transgression of the constitution, then they will file a claim.

"The arbitration panels will have ultimate authority to decide an issue, although an appeals process will be timely and fair as stated in this statute. As for lawyers, sadly they are still needed to represent clients in arbitration cases. There is nowhere in the constitution that forbids their profession. I wanted to outlaw them, but in the interest of fairness, they are needed. Perhaps one day we can eliminate them entirely."

John pointed to the next questioner.

"I assume these arbitration cases are open to the public and everything will be a public record? Will they be televised?"

John contemplated. "I suppose television would be okay in important cases if the DRB or arbitration panel deemed it appropriate. As for being open to the public and on public record, absolutely. The one thing we don't want is a secretive society."

John pressed the remote for the next slide and read it.

Article I

Section 7

DRBs and arbitration panels shall consist of half men and half women. Five of each. A quorum of seven will be needed for making decisions. A majority vote will be used for decisions. Once seven members are present, any DRB or arbitration member will hold stop-work authority if they feel the quorum is insufficient. The DRB and arbitration panel members shall not use their religious beliefs for making government decisions. Instead they will use the principles set forth in the constitution.

John pointed to the next questioner.

"I assume that if there are five women and two men that is sufficient for quorum?"

John nodded. "Yes. However, any member can call a halt to proceedings if they feel the quorum is insufficient to render an unbiased decision."

John pointed to the next questioner.

"Why are seven or eight people sufficient for important decisions?"

"Well," John replied, "Seven could be insufficient. That is why I included the stop work authority. As for eight, that will require a five to three majority for a decision. I think that is satisfactory. After all, we will have an efficient unbiased appeals process."

John pressed the remote for the next slide and read it.

Article I

Section 8

There will be no city or county government. Existing cities will exist in name only. There is only one government which encompasses all of Isabella.

John pointed to the next questioner.

"Will we have government offices in each city? After all, Delano is pretty big."

"That's up to the DRB to decide," John replied. "Hopefully we can use private companies and the Internet for most functions, so that we will not need any remote government offices."

John pointed to the next questioner, who was wearing a T-shirt with the flag of Texas on the front. He was in his forties, which seemed to be about the average age of the audience.

"You see no need for city councils, city boards, or city planners?"

John shook his head. "No, we can do this using paid government volunteers. If we setup Bakersfield in an organized manner, we can leverage that organization for the rest of Isabella."

John pressed the remote for the next slide and read it.

Article II

Section 1

Citizenship is a privilege and not a right. Each
citizen is responsible for themselves and must
hold the values of the community. While each
citizen will be respected as a sovereign soul,
this does not give them the right to disturb
the harmony of the community.

John pointed to the next questioner.

"Does this mean that anyone can lose their citizenship if they
don't hold the values of the community? That seems like a slippery
slope of indoctrination where everyone becomes like-minded
without any diversity or free-thought."

John nodded. "Good point. That could happen. However,
in our new country, each citizen will be responsible for their
behavior. For instance, everyone must serve the community and
everyone must adhere to the constitution. This does not mean that
liberty, fairness, and freedom will be curtailed. Quite the opposite.
People will be respected and their rights will not be infringed.
However, if you disturb the harmony of the community, you
could be banished.

"We will be compassionate, but not to the extent that citizens
or visitors can disturb the harmony of the community. If you want
to just take and take and not give back to the community, then
you could lose your citizenship. This won't be done harshly or
capriciously. No one will be banished without an appeals process."

John pointed to the next questioner.

"I find it interesting that you mention sovereign soul. What
does this imply?"

John smiled. "I knew that would come up. I didn't want to put God in the constitution, but the fact of the matter is that the soul exists. This is not conjecture, but something that millions have experienced. If you gather ten highly evolved humans for a discussion on the soul, you would be amazed at what they would say. Science has not yet proven the soul exists, although when you die you instantly lose 21 grams.

"Millions of highly evolved humans know that the soul exists. For many of them, they have experienced it first hand. There are those who can travel out of their bodies and do soul travel. This is quite common and can be verified by researching soul travel. There are others who can communicate directly with discarnate beings. This ability brings them into close contact with their soul. In fact, if you told them that it was impossible to empirically know their soul, they would consider you a naive and lacking spiritual awareness."

John paused and smiled to let the audience ponder this fact. "The existence of the soul makes each human a sovereign soul. This gives humans inalienable rights. Such as the right to be respected, and the right to be treated as a human being. That is the reason that line is in the constitution."

John pressed the remote. Before he read the slide he thought perhaps he went a bit far with his rant and was afraid to look at Julie to see her expression. Being a metaphysical writer, sometimes John would tell people more than they wanted to hear.

Article II

Section 2

Instead of utilizing a series of laws, the community will rely on a single framework of what is unacceptable behavior. This will be called Disturbing the Harmony of the Community. This catch-all legal requirement will be implemented by the DRBs and arbitration panels. While this may seem counter to the community's credo of fairness, arbitration panels will ensure it is not abused. The guiding principles of the community shall not be infringed.

John pointed to the next questioner.

"What exactly is disturbing the harmony of the community? And who decides?"

"Disturbing the harmony is a catch-all law that will be defined over time by the community. It is the credo for the values of the community. It is what we will allow and not allow. Any citizen can file a complaint against a business or another citizen. The arbitration panels will get to decide what is objectionable. Hopefully, we will create a society that is not too strict and that will allow ample freedom of expression and lifestyle."

John pointed to the next questioner.

"Won't this be arbitrary? Won't we get controversial decisions from various arbitration panels, and controversial laws and decisions from the DRBs? I don't see how this could work without creating a mess."

"Perhaps," John replied, "but not necessarily. As long as everyone follows the guidelines set forth in the constitution, then it can be the constitution that guides us. Sure there will be poor decisions and poor laws, but hopefully these will be the exception. And the way this system is designed, it will be self correcting. Bad laws can be overturned by citizen referendums. Bad DRB decisions and bad arbitration decisions can be appealed. This is a fairer system than our current constitution, that allows influence and power to corrupt politics and justice."

John pressed the remote and read the slide.

Article II

Section 3

> No standing army will exist or be organized. Local militias are allowed to form of their own accord, as long as their objective is for the defense and well being of the community. The only permanent government employees will be police and firefighters. Anyone suspected of violating a law or Disturbing the Harmony of the Community can be reported to the police who will inform the arbitration panels.

John pointed to the next questioner.

"Isn't this article too restrictive? What if we are attacked by an outside aggressor? Can't the DRBs get involved in planning our defense? Can't we get organized?"

"No," John replied. "This is the risk we take. Standing armies are never as effective as we want them to be. If we allow them, then it is only a matter of time before we are at war with someone. In the event we are attacked, the local militias can fight together to defend the country. Without any gun laws, most of the citizens will most likely be armed. It won't be easy for an invader to take us over. We will defend ourselves."

John pointed to the next questioner.

"Why do the police and firefighters get to have permanent positions?"

"The simple answer is tradition. I decided that we needed a symbol of our unity. The men and women who protect us will be that symbol. They will be the only the people who wear the uniform of the country, and we will hopefully be proud of them. They will be the remnants of what once was. They will also symbolize what we cannot go back to—big government."

John pressed the remote and read the slide.

Article II

Section 4

All citizens will be identified as citizens in the government database. This database will include their picture, retinal scan, address, phone number, email, height, weight, and eye color. The government will issue ID cards based on this information, which will be easy to obtain. The data should be updated every 5 years.

John pointed to the next questioner.

"John, I'm not comfortable with government ID cards and government databases. What about our privacy?"

"If we are a community that trusts each other," John began, "then we should want our information to be used in a benevolent way. We all know that today our privacy is abused by businesses and governments. It doesn't have to be that way. The government should be our benevolent benefactor. However, in order for government to work with its citizens, it must know who we are. Notice that this information does not include sex, nationality, race, place of business, etcetera. Its only purpose is to know that its citizens exist and to have their contact and identification information. This data can be used to enforce immigration laws and for efficient citizen voting.

"By stating this in the constitution, it clearly delineates what information will be shared by its citizens with the government. You can have my picture and my identification information, but that's it. You can know who am I, and where I live, but not what I am or what I do. That's personal, private information. Isn't that better than what is happening today? Government today wants to know literally everything about each citizen. It's unbelievable how much information is collected today about each of us. Our work history, financial history, health history, driving history, police records, court records, phone records, internet records, gun records, et cetera are all collected. This new constitution only asks for very basic contact information. Can you compromise?"

The questioner nodded.

John pointed to the next questioner.

"What will the government ID cards be used for, and can anyone query this database?"

"It will be used as a driver's license for one thing. We're not going to have a DMV. Also, as an ID for traveling. And if you want a passport, we can use the government ID as the basis for issuing one. It will be an accepted ID for voting and for obtaining a job. It will have a lot of functions and will be something you will hopefully be proud to own. It will literally be your Isabella citizenship ID card.

"To answer your second question, any citizen can query the database. However, they can only pull up their personal record using a biometric retinal scan. No one will be able to search other citizens' records, unless you provide them with a retinal scan."

John pressed the remote and read the slide.

Article II

Section 5

A citizen can only lose their citizenship if they have been found guilty of a crime or of disturbing the harmony of the community, and have been declared banished. Arbitration boards have the authority to implement 1, 3, or 5-year jail terms, or banishment. If a citizen is banished they will be taken to a random location and released. If they come back, they will be given a 5-year jail term and then banished again. Note that all decisions by arbitration panels can be appealed twice (refer to Article I).

The next questioner was in her youth, perhaps even a teenager. "Why is the maximum jail sentence only five years?"

"Mainly because of economics. We're not going to pay to incarcerate a criminal for more than five years. Crimes that are too egregious for a five-year term will result in banishment. Basically, you lose your citizenship for egregious crimes."

John pointed to the next questioner.

"But is it right to release dangerous criminals into society? Isn't banishment another form of a crime? A crime perpetrated by us? Some people are too dangerous to release."

"I agree," John said. "For those who are truly dangerous to humanity, they will be taken to a desolate island, where they can fend for themselves."

"Okay, let's take a ten minute break. You've been sitting for a while."

John put down his headset and walked over to talk to Julie when a man approached him from the audience.

"John, I've been reading your website and I'm impressed. We need to talk." The stranger was in his sixties and dressed in a suit. He looked like a lawyer or businessman and presented himself as someone confident and successful.

"Julie," John said, "I'll be back in a few minutes."

"Okay," Julie replied.

"Let's go outside and talk," John said.

"What's your name?" John asked, as they walked toward the side door.

"Fred Jackson, but call me Jackson," he said shaking John's hand.

John held the door open as they walked outside to a shady area with a table and chairs.

"What's your story, Jackson?" John asked.

"I want to help you, and I have the resources that can make it happen. My dad left me with considerable real-estate assets and I have parlayed them into successful business investments. I'm ready to spend five or ten million dollars on your plan. My only motive is that I believe in it. I've never supported any politicians or political campaigns, because I think they are all run by crooks and are corrupt. I'm like you, I think the system is completely broken and can't be fixed, and the only answer is to start over.

"I've read your new constitution and I think it's workable. No one else is offering solutions and we are quickly falling into a hole of disrepair. If something isn't done soon, we are going to lose everything: our economic system, our social system, and our political system. I suppose losing those would be a good thing, but not if society devolves into chaos with nothing replacing it but anarchy.

"Your new economic model of removing property taxes and business taxes could literally transform Kern County into a vibrant place to live. I've thought deeply about that and your ideas seem to offer us a way out of this mess we find ourselves. I agree that it's time for action."

John grinned. "I feel like it's my birthday. I'll take your money, but I also want your time, too. I want you to be on the committee that plans the referendum. I'm not offering you this position because of the large donation, nor do I want another dime. You seem to be a highly intelligent person and you obviously have read the new constitution and support it. If you want to make this happen, then come be a part of it."

It was Jackson's turn to grin. "I'm in. When do we start?"

They laughed. "Let's get back inside," John said. "Do you have a card, so I can call you?"

Jackson reached into his wallet and handed John his business card. "I spend about half of my time in Bakersfield, but I can make arrangements to make the meetings."

"Sounds, good," John replied.

They walked back into the conference room. John spoke to Julie and told her some of the details about his talk with Jackson. Then they discussed how the lecture was going and if they needed to change anything. They booth agreed that everything was going smoothly and to keep with the plan.

John put back on his headset and continued with his lecture.

"Okay, everyone find a seat. It's time to resume."

After a short wait, John pressed the remote and read the slide.

Article III

Section 1

Currency shall be gold-backed and convertible into gold. Gold and silver coins shall be accepted as legal tender at the current government spot price. Growth in the money supply shall be limited to a maximum of 3% per year, as determined by the main DRB.

John pointed.

Someone standing up front said, "You stated earlier that there would not be a treasury. Does that mean the DRB will hire a private mint to make the coins and currency? Will the coins be pure gold or pure silver? What will be the gold backing of the currency? One hundred percent, fifty, or what? Who is going to convert dollars or another form of currency into Isabella currency? Will the the new currency float against international currencies?"

John was impressed with this questioner's demeanor and was looking for people who could help him with the referendum. The questioner was young, in his twenties, but was clearly well-spoken and understood several of the issues impacting a new currency. John wanted to talk with him in private.

"Before I begin, can you come talk to me after the lecture? I have a question for you. To answer your questions, yes the DRB will have the money created by private businesses. The silver coins will be pure, but the gold coins will need to have copper and silver for hardening. The percentage of backing will be determined by the DRB. The currency doesn't have to be one hundred percent backed. As long as it is partially backed and convertible that will create enough stability in the currency.

"Convertibility will be handled by private businesses that can set their own fees. If a business will not convert a particular currency into Isabella currency, or vice versa, then the iron hand of the free market will exert its influence. Your California dollars at a certain point might not be convertible. You might not get a penny in Isabella currency for your dollars."

John smiled and several members of the audience laughed at the irony.

John pointed.

"Is the purpose of this statute to prevent inflation and provide stability in prices?"

John nodded. "Indeed. That is exactly what this section is for. In the history of fiat currencies, every one of them has eventually become worthless through inflation. We need to prevent that from happening."

John read the next slide.

Article III

Section 2

Banks, insurance companies, and other finance companies shall all be non-profit. There shall be no stock market, nor any publicly traded companies operating in Isabella.

John pointed.

"This implies that any publicly traded company currently in Kern County must leave. Is that true? And it implies that all financial institutions must switch to non-profit. Is that really fair?"

"Well, publicly traded companies will have options. They can become non-profit or spin-off their operations in Kern County to be non-profit. They can also sell to the highest bidder.

"As to the fairness, this doesn't mean they can't stay in business. A non-profit can make a profit and pay salaries just like a for-profit business. The only difference is that non-profits can only do what they are chartered to do, and their assets cannot be inherited or sold. A non-profit can only be given to another non-profit or given away.

"I suppose if there are any private insurance or financial companies in Kern County, they could file a claim of unfairness and request remuneration for their assets. I made them non-profit so that they could be of service to the community and not pilferers. We need to change the system. Currently if you deposit money in a bank, it might stay there for only twenty-four hours. You give them a dollar and they immediately loan or invest ninety cents of your money. Your dollar is essentially gone and they don't have to pay you back. The government insurance fund might pay you back, but the bank doesn't have to. They can just claim insolvency. That's criminal. We have to end the current banking system, and this is the best method — removing the profit motive."

John pointed.

"So, you are implying that banks will be limited to storing our money in their vaults and they won't be able to make loans?"

John shook his head. "No, that wouldn't serve the public good. People and businesses need to be able to borrow money. The difference this time will be that the non-profit charters will ensure that the reserves at the bank are sufficient to prevent bank runs. I would hope the DRBs use a level of reserves of at least fifty percent of the bank deposits.

"I want to clarify that all decisions by the DRBs and arbitration panels will be public records available on the Internet. All of the non-profit charters will be concisely spelled out and transparent. We won't have hundred-page decisions that no one understands or has time to read. We will keep things simple and easy to understand. If an eighth grader can't understand it, then it needs to be re-written."

John read the next slide.

Article III

Section 3

Business shall use a maximum 25 to 1 pay scale, whereby the top paid employee is paid no more than 25 times the lowest paid. For non-profits, a maximum 10 to 1 pay scale shall be enforced. Any bonus pay or profit sharing will be the same for all employees.

John pointed.

"This implies that bonus pay will be distributed the same way professional sports teams divide championship bonuses. Everyone gets the same amount, unless you missed part of the season."

John nodded. "That is correct."

John pointed.

A middle-aged gentleman with a deep gravelly voice asked, "Can citizens start multiple businesses and get salaries from each one?"

John paused. "I think you found a loophole. I'll think of a way to prevent someone from abusing this statute. We don't want someone to break their corporation into several businesses simply to get paid more."

John read the next slide.

Article III

Section 4

Unions shall be outlawed for both private and public employees. There shall be no collective bargaining. Any injustice or discrimination can be reported to the employment DRB for review.

John pointed.

"What can employees do if they feel underpaid?"

"They can find another job," John replied. "The problem with unions is that they are divisive and cause conflict. A union by definition is created to unite workers against a common opponent. In most cases, the opponent is management, although lately because of the preponderance of government workers forming unions, the opponent has been tax payers. Unions should never be needed. A better solution, one where harmony, integrity, and fairness are the outcome, is what we should strive for.

"A country that allows unions is setting itself up for failure. Why? Because unions will inevitably bleed their opponent dry. This has happened to the multitude of manufacturing plants that have closed over the past century. And it is happening today, with government workers leveraging their union power to slowly bankrupt cities and counties.

"The solution is to outlaw unions and replace them with more equitable and just laws. What is the saying, 'two wrongs don't make a right?' Well, that pretty much sums up unions. Management is wrong to pay workers paltry wages and keep everything for themselves, which is the first wrong. But creating a union to fix this, is also wrong. It might work in the short term, but inevitably it disrupts the business competitiveness, or taxpayer's ability to pay exorbitant salaries and pensions."

John pointed.

"This means the police and firefighters won't be allowed to have unions?"

John nodded. "Correct."

He read the slide.

Article III

Section 5

Inheritance, Gifts, Property, and Real Estate transactions shall be exempt from taxation. The owner of a property shall not be evicted from his property unless an arbitration panel rules in favor of his/her banishment from the community. In the event of banishment, the offender will be paid the current market rate for their property.

John pointed.

"No property taxes or real estate taxes?"

"Nope," John replied. "And property can be bequeathed in a will without any inheritance taxes. Shouldn't a parent be able to give an heir their home without the taxman wanting his annual property tax? Under this system the real owner is the taxman. Today in the U.S. there is not one piece of land that is not taxed. It's criminal, if you ask me. It gives the government power over the people. True freedom requires property rights."

John pointed.

"Is there anything in the constitution to prevent inflation in housing prices? With zero property taxes, a house will be worth a lot of money. We could easily have a housing bubble."

"Yes," John replied. "In Article IV there is a section that prevents investors from making money renting homes, and single family homes from remaining empty. These two statutes should maintain a housing inventory. I suppose it might be a good idea to limit the price per square foot on entry level houses. That might be a good law."

John read the next slide.

Article III

Section 6

A flat tax of 10% on all income will be imposed on all citizens. Businesses will be exempt from income tax. This tax will be due June 1st. It will be paid to a revenue DRB. This DRB will have the authority to assign investigators for irregular tax filings. The main DRB will have the authority to raise this amount in increments of 1%. However, the citizens can overturn this increase (refer to Article I).

John pointed.

"Will there be any exemptions for the poor? And will there be paycheck withholding?"

John shook his head slowly from side to side. "No exemptions. All citizens pay ten percent. And withholding will be optional with no penalties."

John pointed.

"Is there anything to stop taxes from rising to twenty percent or higher?"

John shook his head. "No. We could add a maximum if you think it's needed. I would support twenty percent, but I'm optimistic that it will never get that high. I expect the government to run efficiently and remain small. Over the long term it's hard to predict what will happen. We could start out as a low tax country and become a high tax country. It's the responsibility of the citizens to maintain it.

"I do have a comment for those who would like to see no income tax. After all, the original constitution of the United States prohibited income tax. I've decided to eliminate property taxes and include income taxes. I don't think excise taxes, sales taxes, and fees can raise enough income to finance the needs of the community."

John read the next slide.

Article III

Section 7

A sales tax of 5% will be used for all transactions exchanging goods. There will be exemptions for food, medicine, medical treatment, and real-estate transactions. The main DRB will have the authority to raise this amount in increments of 1%. However, the citizens can overturn this increase (refer to Article I).

John pointed to the next questioner, an elderly lady at least 80 years old, although she appeared in robust health. He wondered why an elderly lady would care about a new constitution. It gave him hope that if she was interested then many other people also had to be interested.

"I'm concerned about tax increases. Why are we going to allow a DRB with the power to increase taxes so easily?"

John replied, "You need to have more trust in the DRB. If inflation is under control, there should not be a need to constantly raise taxes. And the citizens can overturn tax increases with a majority vote."

John pointed.

"How do citizens overturn tax increases?"

John looked closely at the young lady in her early twenties. He was glad to see young people interested in politics and secession. He thought about asking her why she had come today, but decided it was better to stick with the agenda of answering questions.

"It's a two step process. First, there needs to be signatures from ten percent of the registered voters to get the measure on the ballot. Second, a majority vote is required to overturn the law. This is explained in Article One, Sections Four and Five."

John read the next slide.

Article III

Section 8

There will be a 15% tax on overnight accommodations (for room charges), transportation fuel, tobacco, and alcohol. For consumers who pay this tax, there will be no additional sales tax.

John pointed.

"Why so high?"

"Why not?" John replied. "For hotels, most of these taxes will be paid by visitors. If they can't afford the tax, they can stay at lower priced hotel. For transportation fuel, this tax will be a decrease of what we are currently used to. For tobacco and alcohol, I think the tax is well justified."

John pointed.

"I also think it's too high. Why not ten percent?"

"Do you want to pay more income taxes?" John asked. "Because without these taxes, we will not be able to afford a low income tax rate. Many of these taxes will be paid by visitors. Anyone driving through who stops for gas will be paying each of you with these taxes."

John read the next slide.

Article III

Section 9

An employee shall work a maximum of 30 hours per week, with overtime illegal. For those who want to work more hours, they can become a government volunteer or start a business. Business owners and volunteers are exempt from this restriction.

John pointed.

"How will the stores remain open?"

John laughed. "We can make adjustments. If a store owner wants to be closed on weekends, they have that choice. The government is not going to regulate store hours. Hopefully, businesses will hire enough employees to remain open to satisfy their customers."

John pointed.

"This seems utopian to me and impinges on the rights of business owners to run a business."

"I expected some push back on this section from this conservative community," John replied. "However, we are going to change our focus from a consumer-based society that is contingent on economic growth, to one of sustainability and harmony. Making money, getting rich, and obtaining material wealth is no longer the objective. Now we are going to balance our work life with our personal life. We are going to stop being stressed to death and enjoy life."

John read the next slide.

Article III

Section 10

The minimum wage will be considered a living wage, and set by the main DRB annually on January 1st. There are two possible minimum wages for both profit and non-profit businesses. The lowest wage is 10 to 1 for non-profit and 25 to 1 for profit businesses—if it is higher than the annual minimum wage.

John pointed.

"Why have a minimum wage at all? Doesn't this hurt business?"

John paused and reflected. "Many of those who will vote against this constitution will call statutes such as this one un-American. However, do you want to create a country that is safe? Where you can walk at night without worry? A place where its citizens are happy and content and feel like they are treated fairly and given an opportunity to be happy?

"This constitution is ambitious. I will admit that, but it is quite possible to achieve. That won't happen if we don't fix the problems we have. And one of those problems is income inequality and class stratification. Currently the top one percent make an un-godly amount of money, and the lower class barely survives. This statute levels the playing field and raises the income of the lower class. It's fair and needs to be done."

John pointed.

"You don't seem like you are very flexible on this statute."

John nodded. "I'm passionate about fixing the problems, and this is one of the bigger ones that needs to be addressed. Otherwise, we just carry on with the same failed government policies."

John read the next slide.

Article III

Section 11

Both a drivers license and vehicle registration will be free. No physical drivers license is required for driving. However, you must be 18 years old, pass an online written test, and have an adult family member verify that you know how to drive. You can use your Government ID Card for identification. Vehicle registration can be done online, with the registration and license plate mailed to the citizen.

John pointed.

"Isn't this a bit dangerous?"

John shook his head. "No. Remember, an adult family member is responsible for verifying that someone can drive competently. Also, they have to pass a written test. I see no reason to have a DMV. Let's let it die."

A few people applauded.

John pointed.

"What about truck drivers?"

"That is in another section," John replied. "Anyone who requires a professional license must attend training."

John read the next slide.

Article III

Section 12

If there is a budget deficit and additional income is necessary, a 10% business tax can be implemented on income over $1 million, with the first $1 million exempt from tax. Also, an import and/or export tax of 10% is permissible if deemed necessary by the DRB.

John pointed.

"It seems like you are making it too easy for the DRB to increase taxes."

"I consider these emergency taxes," John replied. "It should only be used to balance the budget, and hopefully it is never needed. Like you said, there are many ways the DRB can increase taxes. I am giving them a lot of options so they can be flexible with their decisions."

John pointed.

"What's going to stop them from taxing us to death?"

"The citizens. We have the power to overturn any new law."

John read the next slide.

Article IV

Section 1

No money shall be given to those in need. Instead, assistance will be given directly to those in need. Public housing centers, public food centers, public healthcare centers, and public job training centers will be supported by the government. Free bus rides to these centers will be available to the public.

John pointed.

"Can we afford this with our low tax system? Also, won't these public housing centers deteriorate into ghettos?"

"I'm confident that costs can be contained. My expectation is that these are areas of help and nothing more. They will provide a roof and a bed, basic food, healthcare, and job training. These are not places were the objective is to create a second class community. They are temporary stop-gap centers designed to help someone get back on their feet, and back into the community.

"As for public housing centers deteriorating into poverty conditions, I think we can prevent that from happening. If one of these centers becomes seedy, we can tear it down and build another one nearby. As for crime, these centers will have private security."

John pointed.

"But what about those who have no motivation? Won't they abuse the system and gladly accept handouts?"

"It will be our job as a community to reduce this outcome. In the near term, I would expect a lot of apathy. But as jobs become more widely available, and a better life is offered to those who apply themselves, these centers can become positive social structures. I envision people taking the community bus to these centers simply for job training opportunities."

John read the next slide.

Article IV

Section 2

Public housing centers will be separated into different groupings, such as the short-term homeless, long-term homeless, disabled, and veterans. With the availability of public

housing centers, there will be no need for
sleeping on the streets and loitering in public
places. While some citizens will choose this
lifestyle, it will be required for them to live
in the public housing centers.

John pointed.

"This section seems to outlaw being homeless. Are you going
to jail the homeless if they don't follow this rule?"

John nodded. "Yes, citizens will be required to live in public
housing areas. This statute effectively makes it illegal to sleep
on the streets and loiter in public places. If a citizen continues to
abuse this statute then they could face jail. That is a possibility."

John pointed.

"Why are your guiding principles focused on freedom and
liberty and then this section seems to lack both."

John paused in contemplation. "As a citizen you have a
responsibility to give back to the community and not to disrupt
its harmony. This goes for all citizens, not just those who are
successful. If you find yourself without a home, we as a community
will provide you a safe place to sleep. I think that is a compassionate
approach. All you have to do is take the bus to the public housing
center. At these centers, we will provide food, clothes, showers,
and job training. There won't be any cable TV or smart phones,
nor any entertainment. These centers will not be designed for
sustained living or even a moderate living standard. It will be a
place that you only want to stay on a temporary basis.

"The one exception will be the housing centers for veterans
and the disabled. For these, we will try to create a quality of life
that is not as austere. For the mentally unstable, we will provide
centers with professionals who can help."

John read the next slide.

Article IV

Section 3

The public housing centers will be designed to provide a temporary refuge and not a permanent community. It will only provide the bare necessities and not attempt to create a high quality of life or sustainable living arrangement. The food menu will be austere and the amenities just as austere. Conversely, it should provide free counseling and job training. Those residing in these centers should be given help to get back on their feet.

John pointed.

"I'm guessing that by austere you mean bread, soup, and beans? And not too many desserts? Just enough to live on, but not enough to be comfortable with?"

John nodded. "Exactly. I think you summed it up well. We don't want to create a community out of these centers, but stepping stones."

John pointed.

"Perhaps it would be a good idea to use one of these centers for the chronically homeless. I know it's not the most humane solution, but it might be practical to achieve the goals of the constitution."

"That's not a bad idea," John replied. "I envisioned several of these shelters throughout Isabella. Using one for the chronically homeless might be a good decision."

John read the next slide.

Article IV

Section 4

Any house that has not been lived in for 12 months must be put on the market for sale or sold at auction. Any house on the market for more than 6 months, must be sold at auction. All houses offered at auction, must have an open house for 3 days prior to the auction.

John pointed.

"How do you identify if a house has not been lived in?"

"That should not be difficult," John replied. "The water bill and electrical bill could be used as a preliminary red flag. Then someone could check on the property and contact the owner."

John pointed.

"Why do you want to do this?"

"To contain housing prices and maintain a good inventory of houses," John replied. "With no property taxes, houses are going to be valuable. For this reason, no one is going to want to sell a valuable asset if they don't have to. We have to put something in the constitution to ensure houses do not sit empty."

John read the next slide.

Article IV

Section 5

Single family houses must not be owned for rental income. All Single family rentals must be sold or put up for auction within 6 months of the new constitution. Single family houses will be appraised when the constitution is approved. From that point forward they can only appreciate in value at most 3% per year.

John pointed.

"This statute seems pretty severe. Many people today are getting their livelihood through rental income."

"That's true," John said. "However, with no property taxes we need to take extraordinary measures to prevent housing prices from exploding. Places like London, Vancouver, New York, Melbourne, Vail, et cetera have become so expensive that no one can afford housing except the wealthy. That could easily happen here if we don't prevent it."

John pointed.

"Does this mean if my house appraises for one hundred thousand dollars after the constitution is passed, then the most I can sell if for is one hundred and three thousand a year later?"

John nodded. "Yes, that's the most you can sell it for. You can sell if for less if you don't get any offers."

John read the next slide.

Article IV

Section 6

Multi-unit housing will be allowed as rental properties, although they must be non-profit. All multi-unit housing rental rates will be determined annually by arbitration boards, based on the financial situation of the owner and the current market rates.

John pointed.

"Why do they need to be non-profit?"

John nodded. "Mostly because of greed. Real-estate is an easy way to accumulate wealth, especially in an environment with no property taxes. We need to ensure that housing is affordable and this is the only way to do it—by removing the profit motive."

John pointed.

"Why do we need rent control? Why can't we let the market determine the rental rates?"

"I don't want to take the risk of high rental rates," John replied. "Once rates get high, they never come down. Also, whoever owns an apartment complex is likely doing very well financially. An arbitration panel's decision isn't going hurt them financially. More likely the panel is just going to keep them from squeezing what the market can bear."

John read the next slide.

Article IV

Section 7

All health care related businesses shall be non-profit. This means doctor salaries can be a maximum of 10 times the lowest salary in the organization. Fees charged to patients will be subject to review by the DRB for potential regulation, and excessive charges can be appealed by patients. Health and nutrition shall be taught in high school for at least a single year. The focus of this education will be on preventing disease and staying healthy.

John pointed.

"Doctors, dentists, and ophthalmologists are not going to be happy with this statute."

John smiled. "No, they will not. But we need to lower the cost of healthcare and this is the best way to do it. If a doctor wants to make five hundred thousand dollars, then he can pay his receptionist fifty thousand. We just won't have any doctors making a million dollars a year."

John pointed.

"This seem anti-market to me. Why do you want to impose so much regulation?"

"Because it's healthcare," John replied. "If we want to reduce costs, then we have to remove the profit motive. Is it really necessary to pay fifty thousand dollars for a heart bypass? Or five thousand dollars for a single chemo treatment? If the healthcare industry could be self-regulating, then this statute would not be needed. This constitution limits doctors' salaries and makes both insurance companies and healthcare companies non-profit. That alone will shrink a lot of the costs. But we also need a mechanism in place, in case those structures fail. Hopefully very little regulation will be required.

"We will be importing most of our medicine, so many drug costs will not drop dramatically. However, we will import from all over the world and this will allow us to get the lowest prices. Also, we will try to sign long-term contracts that allow us to get discounts from suppliers."

John read the next slide.

Article V

Section 1

The postal service, cable service, garbage service, phone service, water service, sewer service, maintenance of roads and bridges will be private and awarded to the lowest bidder every 3 years. The DRB can add services to this list if it is in the interest of the community.

John pointed.

"Can there be multiple cable providers, or are we going to use monopolies?"

"That is what the last line is for," John replied. "The DRB has at its discretion the ability to add services in the interest of the community. Furthermore, the citizens can vote to eliminate these services using referendums."

John pointed.

"I take it that some services will be billed to the country and the rest billed directly to citizens. The DRBs will decide?"

John nodded. "Yes."

John read the next slide.

Article V

Section 2

No illegal citizens are allowed to work or reside in Isabella and will be banished if detected. Knowingly hiring an illegal citizen is illegal. All persons living in Isabella prior to the passage of the constitution are eligible to apply for a Government ID Card, which gives them citizenship. A visitor can file for a visa if they plan to stay for longer than 1 year. They can renew this visa if they find work and wish to stay. After 5 years they can request citizenship.

John pointed.

"Where will they be banished to?"

"Most likely their home country. This can be decided by the DRB."

John pointed.

"This implies that anyone can come to Isabella as a visitor and file for a visa and seek work. Won't we get inundated with new arrivals? And can these new arrivals use the public housing centers for room and board?"

"This statute states that they can file for a visa," John replied. "That does not mean they will get one. The DRB can determine how many visas will be issued each year. Also, we are not going to allow illegal citizens. This means visitors cannot use the public housing without a visa."

John read the next slide.

Article V

Section 3

There are no business regulations other than following building codes and honoring the principles of the community. This means polluting the environment will be illegal. A business license is free and can be obtained online. There are no reporting requirements. A citizen in violation of this section can lose their privilege to receive a business license.

John pointed.

"This implies that businesses will be self-regulating. Do you expect employees and citizens to report abuses and misdeeds that are counter to community standards?"

John nodded. "Yes. It will be duty of the citizens to report complacency. We are not going to use paperwork and inspections.

It will be a system of honor. But with self-regulation comes responsibility, and if abuse is detected this could result in fines or the loss of a business license. Severe violators can lose their ability to hold a business license in Isabella."

John pointed.

"Does this mean that their financial records will also be private?"

John nodded. "Yes, private businesses will not have to report their financial records. However, if they get audited it will be necessary to open their books to the auditors."

John read the next slide.

Article V

Section 4

All food products sold inside stores must have labels that include the ingredients. No GMO products can be grown or sold in Isabella. No pharmaceutical drugs can be given to healthy animals intended for food production. No herbicides can be used within a city's borders.

John pointed.

"Are there any regulations for growing food in your front yard or back yard? And can this food be sold to the public?"

"The answer is no to any regulations, and yes to selling to the public. Grow all the food that you can and sell it to your neighbors. We can export any extra food grown in Isabella. We don't have any regulations to prevent this type of activity. Anything that helps a citizen and their family should be supported."

John pointed.

Chapter One: It Begins

"Are we going to impose fines on anyone growing or selling GMO products, or injecting pharmaceutical drugs into their animals?"

"Arbitration panels can decide the penalties and then offenders can appeal twice."

John read the next slide.

Article V

Section 5

No gun laws or drug possession laws shall be created. Except for minors under 21. Industrial hemp farming shall be legal, along with all industrial hemp products.

John pointed.

"No drug possession laws? Does that mean narcotics are legal?"

John shook his head. "No, it's still illegal to sell narcotics. However, buying and possessing drugs is legal. I would prefer not to legislate morality at all, but this community is too conservative. This is the one thing that I thought was acceptable.

"I would prefer to let adults choose how they live and not have the government impose its moral standards on its citizens. But that's not possible. This community doesn't want to legalize drugs, gambling, and prostitution. That's too bad, because ideally adults should be able to choose how they live without the government telling them what is acceptable."

John pointed.

"No gun laws? No gun registration? Anyone can walk into a store and buy a gun? Doesn't this seem dangerous?"

John nodded. "Yes, it is dangerous, and there will be violence. However, this is the only way to protect our community. If we use gun owner registration, then the government or a foreign invader can find the gun owners. The whole point of no gun laws is for the people to be able to protect themselves. Good luck invading Isabella. There is a reason the U.S. Government did not try to prevent Texas from secession—the Texans were armed."

"Let's take another break and then we will come back and finish."

John removed his headset and walked over to Julie. So far the meeting had been going on for two hours.

"How do you think it went?" He asked.

Julie smiled. "You're doing great. I think we probably should have used video, but we can post the audio on Youtube."

John hesitated in contemplation. "Hasn't Jamie done some video work?"

Julie nodded. "Yeah, she could do it."

Jamie worked at Julie's art studio, and was Julie's best friend.

"Why don't you ask her for next time," John said. "And ask if she wants to be on the secession committee. I know she is mostly apolitical, but she cares deeply for humanity and she could be a good addition."

Julie said, "You're serious? Okay, I'll ask her."

John smiled.

A young man in his late twenties approached. "John, you asked me to come see you? I asked a question earlier."

John smiled. "Yes, what's your name?"

"Russell. Russell Simpson," He replied.

"Are you from Kern County? Are you a native?"

"Yes, sir. I am from Bakersfield and I attended Cal State Bakersfield."

"Call me John. I've never liked being called sir. What did you major in?"

"Management Information Systems and Computer Science. I'm a systems analyst for local oil company."

John nodded. "And you're interested in politics? And what's happening in the world? Is that why you're here today?"

"Absolutely. I've spent many hours on your website reading posts. I support your constitution and secession. It's time for a change."

John smiled. "Excellent. This is Julie, my wife."

They shook hands.

"Nice to meet you, Russell," Julie said.

"Likewise," Russell replied.

"Russell, how would you like to be on the committee for secession? I'm looking for someone who is young and is passionate about this subject."

Russell grinned. "I would be honored. If you're asking, then the answer is yes."

"We are going to begin committee meetings in a few weeks," Julie said. "Can you give me your phone number and email and I'll contact you?"

"Sure," Russell replied. He handed her a business card.

"Thank you," Julie said.

John extended his arm to shake Russell's hand. "Okay, well I have to get back to the lecture."

"Thanks, I'll see you at the first meeting," Russell said. He turned and walked back to his seat.

John walked back to where had been lecturing and put on his headset.

"Okay everyone. In a couple of minutes we will resume."

John waited two minutes and then read the next slide.

Article V

Section 6

No fast food chains shall be allowed. No smoking at indoor public places shall be allowed, although private businesses, homes and apartments are exempt.

John pointed.

"If there is a local restaurant with multiple locations, is that acceptable?"

"Most likely," John replied. "However, if someone tries to replace McDonald's with a local chain, I would not expect that to be allowed. The purpose of this statute is to improve the diet and health of the community."

John pointed.

"Are you going to outlaw smoking at public parks, lakes, and trails?"

"No, that is permitted. Only indoor public places are prohibited."

John read the next slide.

Article V

Section 7

Any form of advertising to overturn laws is deemed illegal. Any form of advertising that is deemed to be at odds with the community's well-being is deemed illegal.

John pointed.

"What kind of advertising would be illegal?"

"The first one I can think of is advertising of tobacco or alcohol products. But there are a vast number of borderline issues or products that the DRB could view as harmful to the community's harmony. Television marketing can be quite persuasive and should be regulated to a certain extent.

"For instance, today television commercials bombard you with pharmaceutical drugs, fast food, alcoholic beverages, et cetera. It's a long list of stuff that is bad for you. I'm okay allowing adults to choose what they want, but we shouldn't endorse it. And anyone who thinks that parents have control over their teenager's dietary habits lives in fantasyland."

The crowd laughed.

John pointed.

"Would legal advertisements or healthcare related advertisements be okay?"

"Very likely," John replied, "but these would be at the discretion of both the DRB and any arbitration panel that reviewed a complaint."

John read the next slide.

Article V

Section 8

Natural resource production will be taxed at 75%. Existing publicly traded natural resources companies (oil, natural gas, wind, water) must be sold to private companies within 1 year, or else there will be an auction.

John pointed.

"This seems extreme. This implies that we are going to force publicly traded resource companies to sell at discount prices to private companies."

John nodded. "Texas raised their taxes on oil and natural gas. It's our country. It's our natural resource. Do you want to improve our standard of living, or do you want to continue living like this? Our natural resources are an opportunity waiting to happen. Do we keep that income in the country, or do we let it slip through our fingers?

"Let's look at history. Did you know that at one time the oil in Saudi Arabia was largely owned by western companies? What did Saudi Arabia do? They expropriated it for the people of Saudi Arabia. This is what all of the countries in the Middle East did. Was it wrong? I don't think so. Look at the wealth they accumulated. None of that would have happened if they had given it to corporations for a minor fee and taxable income."

John pointed.

"If we force large oil companies to sell their assets at a discount, won't they sue for damages?"

"Perhaps," John replied "but the world has changed. More and more countries are expropriating natural resources. We are only levying higher taxes. I think that international law will support our right to set our tax rates."

John read the next slide.

Article VI

Section 1

Education shall be the highest priority of the community. Children will get the opportunity for a high quality education. Teachers and principles will be reviewed annually for performance.

John pointed.

"How do we prevent children from failing?"

"We make it a priority," John replied, "and we put a structure in place that ensures that children are educated. This structure is explained in the next two sections."

John pointed.

"I take it you are going to remove tenure because you already outlawed unions. This won't go over very well with our current teachers."

"Our responsibility is not to the teachers, but to the students. If the existing teachers do not want to work without a union, or guaranteed job security, they can find another profession. However, if they are experienced, qualified teachers, then we welcome them to serve the community."

John read the next slide.

Article VI

Section 2

Education will be cost free for students from pre-school through college. However, these will not be public institutions. Instead they will be run by non-profit private companies, with 3-year contracts.

John pointed.

"How can the community afford to pay for private schools? Won't they cost more than our current public school system?"

"We are going to remove a layer of bureaucracy," John replied. "Plus, we are going limit teacher's salaries based on what the community can afford. These non-profit schools can only afford so much in labor costs."

John pointed.

"How can we afford to give a free college education?"

"By using online education," John replied. "This is outlined in section five."

John read the next slide.

Article VI

Section 3

Students and parents can choose which school to attend. They can switch schools at any time. However, problem students can be relegated to specific schools to ensure high quality education for all.

John pointed.

"What happens if the good schools become over-crowded?"

"Schools will be funded on a per-student basis. If a school becomes crowded, they can hire more teachers and add more classrooms. Hopefully we won't face a situation where there simply is not enough room for additional students."

John pointed.

"The last sentence in this statute implies that students can be expelled from certain campuses and relegated to lesser quality schools. Does this mean that the school system will not be standardized and equitable?"

John nodded. "Yes, that is true. It is impossible to have a high level of academics at every school. Some schools will be better than others. However, for any school that is failing, they will be replaced after their three year contract expires."

John read the next slide.

Article VI

Section 4

Students must pass an exam at the 6th grade and 8th grade level to move forward. They must also pass an exam to graduate from high school to become eligible for secondary education.

John pointed.

"Isn't this going to be problematic if students do not pass the test? You are going to end up with older students who could linger for several years."

"It's much more problematic if students are not educated," John replied. "Currently only about half of our students are getting a good education, the rest are relegated to mediocrity at best and illiteracy at worst. This needs to be rectified and this new structure will work. It will force schools to teach their students or else face failure. And the failure will be readily apparent with the students who are stuck in the 6th and 8th grades."

John pointed to the next questioner, a teenager with long hair who looked out of place in a sea of adults.

"At what point do the kids who can't pass the graduation tests get sent home?"

"I'm sure this will happen to some kids who lack learning skills or are simply not motivated," John replied. "Let's just hope that it is a very small minority. Today the illiteracy rate is much higher than is acknowledged. The number of people who cannot write at an 8th grade level is pervasive. With this new system, I think we can get it down to perhaps five percent, and maybe lower with effort."

John read the next slide.

Article VI

Section 5

Secondary education will mostly be performed
online, with face to face educational settings
used out of necessity.

John pointed.

"This is how we are going to limit college costs?"

John nodded. "Yes, and for those parents who want to send
their kids to a brick and mortar school, they can send them to a
school outside Isabella. Online schools are very affordable and
can offer a way for a free college education. All we need to do is
convert Bakersfield College and Cal State Bakersfield into online
schools for ninety percent of their classes. We can use the class
rooms for the few classes that require in-person teaching."

John pointed.

"Do you really believe the quality of education will be
equivalent to that of a brick on mortar school?"

"Sure, why not?" John replied. "Learning is learning. I
will grant you that it won't be as much fun, and that the social
interaction will be lacking. But for a free college education, it will
be a nice option for those who cannot afford to go away to school.
Also, I think online education is the wave of the future, so we are
simply setting the trend."

John read the next slide.

Bill of Rights: Amendments

Amendment 1

Freedom will not be impinged without the
guidelines of the constitution taken into
consideration.

John pointed.

The questioner laughed. "Sorry, but I don't understand this one."

John smiled. "That's because today we don't care if our freedom is constantly squeezed from our lives. This amendment is to ensure that this doesn't happen again. For instance, today we are treated like terrorists when we try to travel. The government collects unbelievable amounts of information about out each of us. They can garner our wages, seize our bank accounts, even imprison us without a legal procedure. They are constantly telling us rule after rule that we have to follow. This amendment basically states to leave us alone, and to not impinge on our freedom unless you have good reason.

"I'm probably aiming a bit high, because this amendment is the essence of freedom, which we probably don't deserve. Once you begin legislating what is acceptable and what isn't, it's a slippery slope to restricting freedom. I don't know about you, but I often feel like a prisoner in my own house."

John pointed.

"What about rules for the public safety, such as speed limits or seat belts laws?"

John smiled. "Of course we'll have traffic safety laws. But we won't have unwarranted searches or imprisonment without a trial, which have both become quite common lately. This amendment tells the government to tread lightly when it comes to restricting freedom."

John read the next slide.

Amendment 2

Spirituality and religion will be a personal matter and not infringed.

John pointed.

"What about *In God We Trust*? Are we going to be an atheist country?"

"Far from it," John replied. "In article two, the soul is firmly entrenched into the constitution. The acknowledgement of the soul is a foundation that society can be based upon. How each individual develops their soul is up to them. It is a personal choice."

John pointed.

"So we are not going to allow prayer or mentioning God's name in schools or government events?"

"If you read the amendment carefully," John replied, "it does not outlaw prayer. It states that someone's preference for religion or spirituality will not be infringed. This basically means that Isabella is not going to be governed by religion."

John read the next slide.

Amendment 3

Freedom of speech and a free press will be protected to the extent that it is not discriminatory or slanderous. No citizen or visitor will be compelled to be a witness or provide information.

John pointed.

"Are we only going to allow speech that is politically correct?"

John sighed. "Total free speech is not possible. As humans we tend to discriminate and verbally attack one another. And until we can overcome this weakness, speech has to be limited. The key is that we do not limit free speech that is critical. A critical voice, as long as it is not discriminatory or slanderous, should be protected."

John pointed.

"Does this mean there will be no political prisoners in Isabella? Will those who discriminate against someone's beliefs be found guilty of a crime? Does this amendment protect witnesses from testifying?"

"The answer to all of your questions is yes," John replied. "There will be no political prisoners. Those who discriminate in any manner could be found guilty of a crime. Citizens are no longer compelled to provide information. All information requested is now voluntary. This means our census will be based on a sample of the population that volunteers information. However, if you want to be a citizen, you must provide contact information."

John read the next slide.

Amendment 4

Citizens and visitors will not be imprisoned without a charge. All will have a hearing by an arbitration panel in a timely manner. There shall not be a death penalty.

John pointed.

"Is this an amendment for habeas corpus?"

John nodded. "Yes, we don't want to allow the government to arrest people and not charge them or give them a trial."

John pointed.

"So, arbitration panels have unlimited power to sentence people to jail, assess fines, or award compensation?"

John nodded. "Yes, they can do what they deem appropriate. I would recommend staying out of trouble. Because if you break the law or the principles of the constitution, a panel is likely to find you guilty."

John read the next slide.

Amendment 5

No citizen or guest will be subject to unlawful searches or seizures. A person's possessions, be they things, records, or ideas shall not be taken without due process of a arbitration panel. A person's physical and mental health shall be protected.

John pointed.

"Does this mean all searches must be approved by an arbitration panel?"

John nodded. "Yes. This may seem extreme, but it is the only way to keep freedom from degrading into an autocracy. It does not mean that an arrest cannot be made, only that an unlawful search is illegal."

John pointed.

"What do you mean by physical or mental health?"

"There are various means of harming both the physical body and the brain. This statute protects both of these. For instance impure food, toxic water, or even strong electronic signals. These will not be allowed, if they are deemed harmful to the human body."

John read the next slide.

Amendment 6

Any form of discrimination is deemed illegal. Impacted parties can seek compensation from arbitration panels.

John pointed.

"Why are you so committed to protecting people's freedom?"

John laughed. "I think it is a worthy goal. Everyone should have the same freedoms. Right to free speech. Right to silence. Right to practice your own form of spirituality. Right to not be discriminated against. Right to fairness. Right to opportunity. Right not to be impinged upon. These are all rights we desire and yet they have eluded us as a society. Now it is time to create a constitution that can provide them — at least on paper."

John pointed.

"Won't we all go crazy trying to create the impossible, which is utopia?"

John smiled. "It's worth trying. It's better than the degradation of society that we have been living through."

John read the next slide.

Amendment 7

Whistleblowers who report infractions to community values will be protected.

John pointed.

"Is this needed? Aren't we already protecting against any form of discrimination?"

"I supposed it isn't, but I want to make a statement that it is okay to be a whistleblower. You don't have to go and hide if you tell the truth."

John pointed.

"But you can't legislate against ostracism."

"That's another reason to include this amendment," John said. "By making it visible and part of the constitution, hopefully more people will speak up. Too often everyone looks the other way out of fear of consequences."

John read the next slide.

Amendment 8

> All citizens have the right to file a grievance
> against another citizen or business. This
> shall be heard by an arbitration panel in a
> timely manner. If the grievance is identified
> as a frivolous complaint, the arbitration panel
> has the authority to side against the plaintiff.

John pointed.

"Where do people file a grievance?"

"The main DRB will need to assemble a group of government volunteers to organize and operate government functions. One of these functions will be to collect filings and send them to the arbitration panels. The volunteers will randomly be selected to serve government for a one year periods."

John pointed.

"What is a timely manner?"

"The DRB can decide, but I would think within ninety days is sufficient for a grievance."

John read the next slide.

Amendment 9

> Citizens can collect signatures from one-third
> of the electorate for a referendum to modify
> the constitution. A two-thirds electorate vote
> is required to pass the referendum.

John pointed.

"Anything in the constitution can be changed in these referendums?"

John nodded. "Yes, that is the purpose of this amendment. Anyone can write their own referendum and attempt to get one-third of the electorate to sign it. If they get enough signatures then the electorate will vote to modify the constitution."

John pointed.

"Can these referendums add new amendments to the constitutions?"

John nodded. "Yes, that is possible."

John read the next slide.

Amendment 10

Medical doctors shall require licenses. Holistic healing practices shall be legal and self-regulated. Pharmaceutical drugs shall be regulated. Health supplements shall be regulated but only for the benefit of consumers. The medical community will be largely self-regulating. A Country website to share information about local medical doctors and holistic practices shall be created and open to the public for posting information.

John pointed.

"Can grievances be filed against local citizens and businesses whose healthcare practices are detrimental to the community?"

John nodded. "These will go through the normal arbitration process. Anyone can file a grievance against any citizen or business. An arbitration panel has the power to fine or close a business. This also applies to supplement providers and pharmaceutical products."

John pointed.

"How much regulation do you envision? Are we going to have something similar to the FDA?"

John reflected. "We have to regulate the healthcare industry to a certain extent or else the safety of the citizens will be impacted. I would hope that we won't have an elaborate government agency that regulates healthcare, such as the FDA. However, we will be vigilant. If there is a product or practice that is dangerous, hopefully it will be identified by regulators or brought to an arbitration panel swiftly. And if any pharmaceutical company blatantly disregards the safety of the public, they will be banned from selling products in Isabella."

John read the next slide.

Amendment 11

If the citizens overturn a law, the current DRB cannot create a similar law in the same year. If they do so, a citizen can file a grievance to revoke the law, which will go to an arbitration panel.

John pointed.

"What is this for?"

"Without it, the DRB can simply turn around and create a modified version of the law the next day after the vote."

John pointed.

"What's going to stop the DRB from constantly creating new laws?"

"The citizens. If ten percent do not like a law, they can get it on the ballot for a vote to overturn it."

John read the next slide.

Amendment 12

A DRB member can be recalled by an Arbitration panel for unsuitable behavior. A decision in favor of a recall can be appealed twice. If a DRB member is recalled, they will be replaced by an appointment of the remaining members.

John pointed.

"What is unsuitable behavior?

"The obvious one would be taking bribes. However, this amendment allows any citizen to question the actions of DRB members. It could be used to recall the entire DRB if they were making unpopular decisions."

John pointed.

"So, this is to prevent corruption or special interests from controlling a DRB?"

John nodded. "Yes, for instance if there is any suspicion of a DRB member getting paid to vote a certain way, a citizen could file a complaint, which would be heard by an Arbitration panel."

John pressed the remote and the screen displayed *Questions?* He looked at his watch and then scanned the audience. He had been up there for nearly four hours. He was tired and was ready to stop, but he knew the audience likely had a few more questions they wanted to ask.

"We have time for some additional questions. If there is something you would like to ask, please form a line over in the right aisle. Julie has a microphone for you."

Julie raised her hand holding a microphone. Soon there were about ten people lined up.

Julie handed the first person in line her microphone.

"John, I have a question about traffic laws. Are we going to have seatbelt laws, and the same speed limits that we have today? And what about photo enforcement tickets?"

"The DRB can decide these issues and citizens can override their decisions if necessary. I would expect the DRB to determine the fines for various infractions. Most likely a traffic fine will arrive in the mail or via email. If you feel that you were unjustly ticketed, then you can file a grievance, which will be taken up by an arbitration panel. This will all be very simple to carry out. As for photo enforcement, I hope we don't have that. I've always felt that camera tickets were an abuse of our rights. What's next, direct monitoring of our speedometer?"

Julie handed the microphone to the next person in line.

"You seem to take a libertarian attitude. Is that your philosophy?"

"No, not really," John replied. "I like the libertarian ideals of freedom and liberty, but I think government has a place. Without a strong government hand, society will become a mess with the have's dominating the have-nots. In this constitution, you will find a strong hand of both libertarian ideals and a strong government that enforces the principles of the constitution. While the government will not be very big, it will still have the power to enforce the law. It will not be a hands-off government. If citizens think they can trample on the principles of the constitution, they will find themselves in trouble. They will find out that citizenship is a privilege and not a right."

Julie handed the microphone to the next person in line.

"Part of the Monterey oil shale deposit is located in Kern County. Are we going to develop it?"

John hesitated. "That's a tough question. Under this constitution it could be ruled illegal if it is deemed to be polluting the ground water. Being an agriculture community, our ground water is literally our life blood, and we have to protect it. I personally would be very leery of taking that risk."

Julie handed the microphone to the next person in line.

"What kind of drug laws are we going to enforce? Are we going to continue the war on drugs?"

"Again, that's up to the DRB. I'm hoping that first offenses for trafficking in narcotics are lenient. Perhaps two years would be sufficient to give someone time to think about changing their lifestyle. We have to be careful and not end up with a prison population that has a large number of drug-related offenders. After all, drugs are largely a lifestyle choice and not necessarily criminal behavior.

"Since I am talking about prison, I would prefer not to incarcerate white collar criminals. Instead, we should just take away all of their assets. For those white collar criminals who don't have any assets, we could encumber their future earnings. The key to prevention is taking away their incentive to commit a white collar crime."

Julie handed the microphone to the next person in line.

"For education, are we going to set any standards for the private schools that we fund?"

"Only for the sixth grade and eight grade exit exams," John replied. "The whole purpose of using private schools is so that they compete against each other. They need the freedom to set their own standards and their own curriculum. Each school will have three-year contracts. If they do not succeed in educating our children, their contracts will be given to another company. Remember, the children will be our eyes and ears. They will let us know if a school is succeeding or failing. Parents will know. Also, we will have access to the test scores. We will know how schools are performing."

The next person asked, "If citizens want a new law, how do we get the DRB to create one?"

"There are many ways," John replied. "You can write them a letter. You can create a Facebook page or a Meetup group. You can get others to write letters. Use your imagination. While citizens do not vote for new laws, they can try to get a referendum on the ballot to modify the constitution. Modifying the constitution requires a two-thirds vote of the electorate, so that is not easy to do. A new law only requires six DRB members to vote yes, which is much easier to accomplish.

"We are out of time," John said. "For those who did not get to ask a question, please post your questions on my website and I will answer them. We will do this again in month or two. Thank you for coming."

John removed his headset and walked toward Julie. Before he could get to her, a crowd of people approached him with questions.

John held out his hands. He was tired and ready to leave. "I'm sorry, but I can't answer any more questions today. Please use my website or send me an email. I have to go."

John walked around the group and made his way to Julie.

"Let's sneak out," John said. "Or else I'll be answering questions for another hour."

Julie smiled. "Follow me."

They walked out a side entrance and headed for their car.

"The audience was very receptive tonight," Julie said, "They seemed hungry for this message."

"I agree. I think this might happen."

John reflected on how momentous this night had been. When he wrote the constitution and created the website, he thought it might grab some interest, but never envisioned it turning into a large movement. Now he thought it actually had a chance to succeed. They both got into the car. John drove.

"Where do you want to eat?" he asked.

"How about Woolgrowers?"

"Sure."

They drove to East 19th street hoping the wait wouldn't be too long. Luckily for them there was an open table in the front. They sat down and both ordered "the setup", which included everything but an entree. At Basque restaurants in Bakersfield you had to be careful how much you ate or else you would be uncomfortable afterward. You could get full on the soup, beans, and Pyrenees French bread alone.

"When do you think we should have our first committee meeting?" John asked, as he scooped pinto beans into his cabbage soup.

"I was thinking more about where than when," Julie replied.

"How about Frank and Jackie's? They have a big house?"

Frank and Jackie were two of their closest friends. They were local lawyers and the four of them spent a lot of time together on weekends. They were practically family. All of them were of a similar age and neither couple had any children. They were keen to the topic of politics and what was happening in the world. They spent many an evening talking until the late hours about what was wrong with the world.

Julie said, "But this is going to take some time and Jackie might not want the intrusion. I was thinking maybe we should find a business meeting room and make it more formal."

"That's a good idea, but where?"

"We've asked seven people to join the committee. We can ask them. Maybe they will know somebody."

John smiled. "Actually it's eight. I told you at the break that I asked Fred Jackson to join the committee. What I didn't tell you was that he also wants to give us five to ten million dollars ..."

"What?" Julie interrupted.

"Yeah, he's a local and he wants to back what we are doing. I told him that if he was going to invest that much money that he should be more involved. He was game for joining. I like him a lot. He is a very smart guy with a good character, at least that was my impression. He spends about half of his time on business trips away from Bakersfield. He might miss a few meetings, but he told me he would make it a priority to attend."

"That's a lot of money, John."

"We'll spend it wisely."

"Okay, I'll contact everyone on the committee and ask around for a meeting place. John, you need to find us two more people for the committee. We need ten. It's symbolic of the constitution and the size of the DRBs and arbitration panels."

"That's easy. Let's add Albert and Terry. They're good friends and I trust them. Plus, they are both very bright and understand the political system."

Julie nodded. "Yes, they are good choices."

CHAPTER TWO: THE COMMITTEE

John called Charlie and asked him to come over before the first committee meeting. He wanted to discuss an important matter that they could keep between themselves. After their talk they could go to the meeting together.

Julie was at her studio painting and would see them at the meeting.

John heard the knock and greeted Charlie with a smile.

"How's it going?" John asked.

"Good. You?"

"I'm doing well. Come in, we need to talk."

Charlie was a close childhood friend. They trusted each other like brothers. He was a local farmer in the nearby Shafter area, but lived in Bakersfield. Charlie wore a goatee and liked to dress like an Okie, which the Bakersfield area was known for since the Depression in the 1930s. This included wearing a long sleeve printed Western shirt, Wrangler jeans, and cowboy boots. If you judged him by his dress you would have underestimated him. He was college graduate from USC and ran his farm with extreme efficiency.

They both sat down in the living room.

"Thirsty? Want something to drink?" John asked.

"What kind of beer do you have?"

"Corona."

"Okay, I'll take one."

John brought Charlie back a bottle of Corona.

"We're going to do this thing? A referendum?" Charlie asked.

"Yeah. There's no stopping it now. That's why I wanted to talk to you. Jackson wired five million into the account I setup for the committee. However, he also wired another five million into a special account that only he and I know about. I want you to spend some of it."

"On what?"

"Camping supplies. Tents, sleeping bags, food, water, clothes, toothpaste, et cetera."

Charlie was surprised and raised his eyebrows. "What for?"

"There is no way California is going to let us implement the constitution I have written. If the referendum gets on the ballot and passes, they are likely going to bring in the California National Guard and stop us."

"So what's our play?" Charlie asked.

"There is only one, civil disobedience," John replied. "I have a plan that I think might work, so we might as well start preparing now."

"That's what the supplies are for?"

John nodded. "We need enough to supply four thousand people for at least three months. My plan is to occupy Jastro Park and Beach Park, and surround the County Administration Building and the Bakersfield Courthouse during the day."

"You're going to try to shutdown the county government?" Charlie asked incredulously.

"No only me," John replied. "The people of Kern County."

Charlie contemplated. "I hate to agree with you, but I think you might be right. California could use force to prevent us from seceding. We have too much oil and too much agriculture. The lost tax revenue would cripple California."

John nodded. "That's right. And now we can start preparing for that outcome if the referendum passes."

"I'll help. Whatever you need, John." Charlie looked at John with a serious expression.

"I thought I could count on you. I didn't want the other committee members to be involved yet in planning civil disobedience. They will have enough work just to get the referendum on the ballot. In fact, I didn't want us to be involved, but if the referendum passes and they tell us no, I can't accept that outcome."

"What do you want me to do?" Charlie asked.

"Here, write it down." He handed Charlie a notepad and pen.

Charlie grabbed the pen and opened the notepad to the first page.

"Create a list of supplies for four thousand people to camp at Jastro Park and Beach Park for three months. Find someone who can obtain these supplies and work closely with them to finish the job. We need someone with a good business mind. We don't want to pay retail, so someone is going to have to set up businesses and order supplies in large quantities. Any idea who could handle that?"

Charlie looked up at John. "Jimmy Smith would be perfect. He owns about three different businesses and is always looking for opportunities. I'll go talk to him. If we offer him a nice fee, I'm sure he will do it."

"Tell him to put the supplies in storage units that are in a close proximity to downtown. The food should go into climate controlled storage."

Charlie nodded as he took more notes. "Do I have a budget?"

"No, spend what you need." John passed him a card. "Here is the bank and the account number. You are authorized to make withdrawals."

"Anything else?" Charlie asked.

"Yeah, one last thing. I want you to begin renting houses and apartments around Jastro Park. We can use them for their bathrooms and showers. Rent about fifteen. That should be enough."

Charlie nodded and wrote down his final notes. "I'll try. It's not going to be easy finding that many rentals near the park."

* * * * *

Julie was right. It was easy to find someone who had a business conference room they could use. She posted on John's forum and found someone who would donate a room. While her art gallery consumed most of her time, she did find time after hours to help. This was much more John's project, but she was passionate about helping humanity. She would support John in any way that she could. This was her second job and she was devoted to see it through.

When Charlie and John arrived, everyone was already there. Since this was the first committee meeting they had to spend time on introductions. They went around the table and each person talked about their background and why they wanted to be on the committee.

"My name is Susan Johnson. I'm a CFO for Mercy Hospital. I've been in this position for ten years. Before that I was a CPA for a local accounting firm for fifteen years. I'm married with two delightful daughters. I'm here because I want to help. Society is not getting better and we need to do something different. I like this constitution and I think it will work."

"I'm Russell. I don't feel like I'm worthy to be here. Obviously, I'm the youngest by at least a decade. John invited me and I couldn't turn down the opportunity. I'm a computer systems analyst. So I suppose I will be the data gathering arm of the committee. Also my minor in college was political science and I have studied the history of political systems. So I should be able to add a few insights. Oh, I'm single, but I have a girlfriend named Kate.

The committee members smiled. They liked Russell's candor and ease.

"My name is Fred Jackson, but I prefer to be called Jackson. I'm a local businessman, but I spend a lot of time outside Bakersfield for my companies. When I found John's website, I was taken with the constitution. I think we all agree that society has degraded to the point of no return, otherwise we wouldn't be here tonight. The problems are so ingrained into society that we have to start over. His constitution is a very good blueprint for that change."

"I'm Charlie. I farm almonds in Shafter. My family's been farming in the Kern County area since the early 1900s. I'm here because I am a close friend of John's and we have known each other most of our life. I don't especially want to implement this new constitution. I would prefer to continue with our current government. I'm a conservative farmer and I don't like change. However, we're going broke and the economy is a shambles and we have to do something."

"I'm Terry. I'm a small business owner here in Bakersfield. John and I are close friends. We have been discussing the state of the world and state of the economy since 2004, when we met. Many of the ideas in his constitution we have discussed in detail."

Terry was a big man who looked like he probably played football when he was younger. He had blonde hair and blue eyes and had an unusual hobby for someone with his large frame, of running long distance.

"My name is Albert. It looks like I get to be the minority representative for the committee. I'm a history and political science teacher at Highland High School. I've known John all of my life. We hold similar beliefs and there is nothing in the constitution that I object to. Unlike Charlie, I have no problem dismantling the current system and starting over."

Albert was in his mid thirties. He was a deep thinker and was quick to question anyone who thought they understood a subject but in reality didn't have a clue.

Everyone smiled.

"I'm Jackie. This is my husband Frank next to me. We are both local attorneys. It's somewhat ironic that Frank and I are on the committee considering that lawyers are not one of John's favorite groups. However, we have known John for many years and are good friends. He wanted us on the committee to help communicate with the County Board of Supervisors, and perhaps with any legal issues that might arise regarding the referendum."

"I'm Frank. Jackie and I are both huge supporters of the proposed constitution. If this is going to ruin our careers, we are willing to take that risk. Something needs to change before society degrades any further. For those of you who have not considered the ramifications of being on this committee, we will all become full-blown celebrities very shortly. This is likely going to go national, and our names are going to be on the front page of *The Bakersfield Californian* quite often, as well as the local news. If your place of employment can fire you, it might happen."

"Frank is right," John said. "If there is anyone who wants to opt out know, we will all understand."

Everyone looked around the table looking for who would be first to get up and leave, but nobody got up.

"Good," John said. "I thought I had a sturdy bunch."

"I'm Jamie. I am a graphics artist and holistic healer. I am the oddball in the group, and I'm not sure why John and Julie wanted me to be on the committee. I don't care much about politics, but I care deeply for humanity and creating a more peaceful planet. I work with Julie and we are very close friends."

Jamie looked at Julie sitting next to her.

"Everyone should know me. I'm John's wife, Julie. I'm an artist and political activist. This constitution is something I believe in. I want it as much as John, although he is the architect and it's his vision. But I feel that we are a team and are doing this together.

Now you are part of our team. I'm glad everyone is here and I welcome you all. This is going to be difficult to achieve, but one way or another we are going to make history."

Everyone was quiet as Julie looked into the eyes of each of the committee members seated around the table.

"Okay, order of business," John said. "Tonight I want to review the constitution. What did I leave out and what would you like to change? Any changes or additions need to have a majority vote. And I want to clarify one thing, until the referendum passes, any changes or additions to the constitution will require six votes and I need to be present. Is that agreed upon?"

Everyone nodded.

"I'll take silence as a yes," John said. "Okay, who wants to go first?"

"Thomas Jefferson was my favorite founding father," Albert said, looking down at his notes on the table. "I would like to include some of his words in the declaration. Two in particular. First the quote, 'We hold these truths to be self-evident, that all men are created equal, that they are endowed by their Creator with certain unalienable Rights'. And then also the quote, 'When a government fails to protect those rights, it is not only the right, but also the duty of the people to overthrow that government.'"

John turned on the large screen projector and logged onto the laptop in front of him. He did a quick search for Thomas Jefferson and the Declaration of Independence, and displayed the following:

> *We hold these truths to be self-evident, that all men are created equal, that they are endowed by their Creator with certain unalienable Rights, that among these are Life, Liberty and the pursuit of Happiness.—That to secure these rights, Governments are instituted among Men, deriving their just powers from the consent*

*of the governed,—That whenever any Form
of Government becomes destructive of these
ends, it is the Right of the People to alter or to
abolish it, and to institute new Government.*

"I have an idea," John said. "Let's modify this quote and include it as the preamble."

He started typing and then displayed the preamble on the screen. "How about this?"

Preamble

We hold these truths to be self-evident, that all men are created equal, that they are endowed by their Creator with certain unalienable Rights, that among these are Life, Liberty, Justice and the Sovereignty of the soul. To secure these God-given rights, Governments are instituted among Men, deriving their just powers from the consent of the governed. Whenever any Form of Government becomes destructive of these ends, it is the Right of the People to alter or to abolish it, and to institute a new Government.

Everyone was silent as they read the preamble and reflected.

"I like it, although do we need to include the soul?" Albert asked?

John wanted to reply, but stayed silent to let the others discuss the issue.

"I understand what John is trying to achieve here," Susan said. "The soul is what gives each individual their basic rights. We are not entitled to equality, liberty, and justice because of what is written in a constitution. It's much bigger than that. The soul is what makes each person special and why they should be treated with dignity and respect."

"I agree, completely," Fred said. "I know the soul is a big word and can't easily be defined or understood. But what Susan explained is absolutely true. It's the soul that gives each person their identity and specialness. Stating it in the preamble makes perfect sense to me. It's what the country should be based on, and it provides a solid foundation."

"I can't argue with that," Terry said.

Frank, Jackie, and Charlie all nodded.

"I vote yes," Russell said.

"Okay," John said. "Those in favor raise your hands."

Everyone raised their hand, even Albert. John smiled realizing that the group he had formed were all in agreement about something he believed in so strongly. He felt confident that he had picked the right team.

"The change has passed. Who else has a suggestion?"

"I think we should use tolls on Highway 99, Highway 58, and Interstate 5," Charlie said. "That income could be used to maintain the freeways and roads. After all, why should we give away our roads for free to interstate commerce?"

"I agree," Terry said. "Let's charge five dollars for entry into Isabella at the entry points for these three interstate highways. We won't charge for leaving to make it seem fair. If we charge for entry and exit, we won't have a good reputation."

"I can support that," John said. "But let's be explicit that those are the only permitted tolls in the country."

John started typing. I'm going to put it in Article three section thirteen. He displayed it on the big screen.

Article III

Section 13

The only permitted tolls in the County will be on Highway 99, Highway 58, and Interstate 5. It is recommended to only collect an entry toll and not an exit toll. This money will be used to maintain roads and bridges.

"Look good?" John asked.

Everyone nodded.

"All in favor?"

Everyone raised a hand.

"The change is approved. Who's next?"

"What about car smog?" Jamie asked. "We don't want air pollution to get out of control in the valley. We already have some of the poorest air quality in the nation."

"This can be handled by the DRB," John said. "All cars today have catalytic converters and electric cars are becoming more common. If air pollution increases, the DRB can institute something. I don't see a need to put it in the constitution."

"Also, polluting is already illegal in the constitution," Susan said.

John looked at Jamie and Julie. "If you can think of something you want us to vote on, we are willing."

"Okay, then I have something," Julie said. "I would like to require a permit to release carbon into the atmosphere. Vehicles that meet certain standards would be exempt. And tolls will be double for vehicles out of compliance."

"The problem with this law," John said, "is that it gives zealots a reason to block the referendum. They will label us as global warming revolutionaries. It's not worth the blowback."

"It's not a bad idea," Jackson said, "but I'm with John. Let's have the DRBs deal with it."

There was silence.

"Okay, let's vote," John said. "Those in favor?"

Only three hands went up. Jackie, Julie, and Jamie.

"The amendment fails. Who's next?"

"I would like to have a millionaire's tax," Jamie said. "And maybe even an asset tax."

John looked at Jamie. "I have made this constitution more fair and equitable than anything that exists on the planet. There is no need to make it toxic. If we include additional taxes for the wealthy, we are creating a very powerful enemy. As the new constitution is currently written they are not going to be thrilled, but they can live with it. I'm lowering their taxes dramatically and allowing them to own their properties free and clear. Conversely, I'm making them share their profits with their employees."

"I agree with John," Jackson said. "It's a bad idea."

"Those in favor of a millionaire's tax?" John asked.

Only Jamie raised her hand.

"Who's next?" John asked.

"I have one," Terry said. "I would like to allow retired policemen and firemen to be able to volunteer to work part-time until they are seventy-five. Many of these people retire in their fifties, but would still like to work part-time."

"Sure, we can add that. Any objections?" John asked.

There was silence.

"All in favor?"

Everyone raised a hand.

John started typing. "I put it at the bottom of article six." He displayed it on the big screen.

Article VI

Section 6

Police and firefighters will have the option to volunteer after retirement to work part-time until they are 75 years of age. Their maximum weekly hours will be determined by the DRB.

"Look good?" John asked.

"Who's next?"

"I think we should legalize drugs, and perhaps even gambling and prostitution," Frank said. "I don't think it's right for the government to tell me how I should live."

Susan shook her head. "If this was a more liberal county, then perhaps I would agree with you. But Bakersfield is not ready to accept any of these lifestyle choices."

Frank looked at Susan. "Prostitution is one of the oldest professions and it is not going away anytime soon. I understand you are trying to protect the degradation of women, but if that's the case, then we should outlaw strip clubs and pornography, and we know that's not possible."

"Maybe there is a middle ground," Russell said. "I was in Perth, Australia a few years ago and a friend pointed out a brothel. I replied that I didn't know prostitution was legal in Australia. He said it wasn't legal, they just didn't enforce the law. Basically the authorities came to the conclusion that prostitution was a necessary outlet for many men. They considered it a humane necessity."

"I agree with Frank's argument," John said, "because I don't want to legislate morality. True liberty means that each adult can make up their own mind how to live their lives. Once we begin deciding what is acceptable for others, we are going down a slippery slope. However, I also agree with Susan. Bakersfield and Kern County are not ready to legalize any of these behaviors."

Jamie looked at Frank. "What about sex slaves and those who make money trafficking humans?"

"That clearly crosses the boundary of disrupting the harmony of the community. Anyone who forces a woman to be prostitute is clearly breaking the law." Frank replied.

"Or man," Jamie replied. "You are legalizing this for both sexes."

"Prostitution is not something I want to condone," Frank said. "But as a libertarian I have to support it."

"Let's vote," John said. "Those in favor of legalizing prostitution?"

Only Frank raised his hand.

"The amendment fails," John said. "Frank do you want to have a vote on legalized drugs or gambling?"

Frank shook his head. "No, it's a losing battle."

"Who's next?" John asked.

"I think we should regulate the militias," Susan said. "If we let them organize freely without any controls they could easily takeover the country using guns and coercion."

"A coup d'etat?" Russell asked.

"Why not?" Susan asked. "We are going to become an independent country. A few thousand armed men could easily takeover."

John looked at Susan. "I'm not going to deny that such an outcome is possible, however the strength of the militias is their anonymity. By regulating these groups, they become an extension of the government. It becomes a self defeating strategy. If we are ever attacked, all our enemy will need to do is obtain the records of the militias and hunt them down. Their secrecy and anonymity is what makes them strong."

"Susan, he's right," Charlie said. "They have to stay hidden."

"The unseen hand of freedom," Terry said.

"Okay, let's vote," John said. "Those in favor?"

Susan, Julie, and Jamie raised their hands.

"The amendment fails. Who's next?"

"I think the drug possession law might be too lenient," Julie said. "I know you don't want to legislate morality, but we also don't want to create a drug culture where permissiveness leads to excess."

"I agree," Susan said. "If we allow narcotics to be legally possessed, we are asking for problems."

"Your argument is that we are going to encourage illegal drug use?" John asked.

Susan nodded. "Yes, if possession is legal, then that encourages drug use."

"Perhaps, but that is the choice of each citizen," John said.

"I think this statute could create a society where drugs are pervasive," Julie said.

"We already have one," Russell replied. "You are implying that if we eliminate legalized possession from the constitution that the drug culture will go away. If that were true, then I would agree with you. However, the drug culture is alive and well. What John has done with this statute is allow adults to make their own decisions without retribution. Drugs are part of our culture and adults should have the right to partake in them if they wish."

John nodded. "Julie, you can't solve the drug problem by keeping possession illegal. It can only be solved by a spiritually aware community. People only avoid drugs when they see that it is not in their best interest. Sometimes experimentation is necessary to learn that lesson. This statute allows people to experiment without retribution."

"I never thought of it like that," Jamie said. "You make a very good argument."

"Okay, let's vote," John said. "Those in favor of making drug possession illegal?"

Susan and Julie raised their hands.

"The amendment fails. Who's next?"

"We should restrict oil production to extend the life of the wells," Terry said. "Instead of producing full out, we should only produce a percentage of the reserves."

"What did you have in mind?" Frank asked.

"I would suggest cutting production by fifty percent and then maintain that production for the next decade. At that time reassess the production rate."

"Essentially, you are trying to double the length of time until we run out of oil?" John asked

"Yeah, something like that," Terry replied. "Right now we have enough reserves for about twenty years at current production rates. We can double that to forty years at half our current production."

"But what if there is a replacement for oil?" Frank asked. "Then we lose all of that money."

"Why not be prudent?" Terry asked. "So what if we lose a little bit of tax money? We can have affordable transportation fuel for forty or fifty more years."

"There's another issue to consider. If we cut production in half, a lot of people are going to lose their jobs. And those are high paying jobs. Also, tax revenues will drop substantially." John said.

"How about seventy-five percent?" Frank asked. "That should only have a marginal impact on jobs, and could buy us another ten years of production."

"I'll second that idea," John said.

"I'll third it," Albert said.

"Okay, let's vote. All those in favor?"

Everyone raised a hand.

"Give me a minute to write it up," John said. After a few minutes he displayed it on the screen.

"I put it in article five, section nine."

Article V

Section 9

Oil production will be reduced to 75 percent of capacity for 10 years. After this, production capacity will be reassessed. The purpose of this reduction is to extend the production life of the wells in order to maintain affordable transportation fuel for Isabella.

"I think that's enough for tonight. Next week we will spend more time on the constitution. I would like to lock it down so that we can move forward with our referendum plans."

CHAPTER THREE: THE INTERVIEWS

A few days later a reporter from *The Bakersfield Californian*, called for an interview. John agreed to sit down at his house. This was exactly what he needed to get the referendum in motion. He wondered if the paper realized that they would create a huge story. Once Kern County started down the road to a referendum, it would be hard to stop. It would take on a life of its own.

Pam Simpson from the *Californian* arrived in the afternoon. She came by herself when John was alone. Julie was at her studio, where she spent most of her time. (Julie loved her work and rarely took a day off during the week.)

"Please, have a seat," John said.

The cat didn't wake from her nap as they sat down to talk.

"Can I record?" Pam asked.

"Sure, you can even post it on the Internet if you want," John replied.

She laughed. "No, it's only for my notes."

"It's a big topic," John said. "How many words are they going to give you?"

"Well, I'm hoping to make it a series. I read your constitution and I was at your Meetup lecture. You seem to have quite a following. It took me some time to get our editors interested, but I convinced them that this is too big a story to ignore."

John grinned. "You were right to force the issue. If you don't do the story first, another paper will be knocking at my door soon. This isn't going away."

"Do you really believe a Kern County secession referendum is possible?"

He nodded. "Look what's happening. The country has already split up and Humboldt County is going to form its own country. After that happens, Kern County is in play. Anything is possible. My new constitution is exactly what we need to revitalize the area."

"But your constitution is radical," Pam said. "It has very little in common with our current government structure. Why do you think people will support it?"

"Because it can solve all of our problems. Our political system isn't working. It's become dysfunctional and manipulated by money. Clearly we need change, so why not start over? There are no jobs to be found and the economy is stagnating. This can be solved by eliminating business taxes and lowering the income tax rate to a ten percent flat tax. Next, we have an income inequality problem. I solve this by no longer allowing privately traded companies to own businesses in Kern County, and create a flatter pay scale with all bonuses paid equally among employees. Then we have an education problem. I address this by making all schools privately run, using three year contracts, and by requiring students to pass exit exams to graduate from the 6th and 8th grades."

"I will admit you have a lot suggestions for our problems," Pam said. "It's quite impressive, but most of your solutions are quite radical. For instance you want to tax oil and natural gas production at seventy-five percent. That's not exactly a free market system."

"If we've learned one thing from capitalism, it's that it must be regulated. A totally free market system creates unintended consequences, and does not result in a harmonious society. The question is how do you re-organize the economy? Natural resources should be owned by the people, yet all of our oil income is leaving the county. It is currently about $10 billion per year in Kern County. That is huge, and nearly all of it is exported.

"The constitution calls for Isabella to receive seventy-five percent of the profits and the private company that owns the oil fields keep twenty-five percent. I think that's fair. They will get billions of dollars in income. Most of which, will go to local Isabellan employees. The difference in this type of economic organization is that most of the profits will stay local, and they will be used to fund the government. It's better than paying high taxes."

"Why go after the oil companies?" Pam asked.

"Because oil is our natural resource. If we don't tax the oil companies, then they are going to take all of their profits out of the county. We can't have that when everyone is hurting economically. We need to keep that money here, locally. This is the solution to that problem."

Pam pushed the recorder a few inches closer to John. "Your constitution replaces politicians with paid volunteers who serve one year terms. There are no elections and no citizen votes, except to overturn laws that voters reject from DRBs or to modify the constitution. Exactly what are these DRBs?"

"Decision Review Boards that consist of five men and five women. There is a main DRB that makes the laws and creates other DRBs and arbitration panels as needed. Any law created by the DRB can be overturned by the electorate."

Pam was skeptical. "So, ten random people get to make all of the laws?"

"No, the first DRB will be elected. Then that DRB gets to appoint their successors. You can only serve once every five years, so there is no revolving door. This constitution attempts to make government extremely small, yet effective. It attempts to keep laws to a minimum. The DRB is not supposed to create laws unless they are necessary. The need for a new law should be so blatantly obvious that any ten qualified people can write the law."

"You want to legalize drug possession," Pam said skeptically. "Why do think that will be embraced in conservative Kern County?"

"The citizens have the right to have this statute removed from constitution. I think it makes sense from a libertarian viewpoint. Adults and not the government should decide how they are going to live. I'm trying to create a country where freedom and liberty are respected, and I don't to want to legislate morality."

"If you don't legislate morality you get immorality," Pam said.

"Perhaps. But you can never eliminate drug use. You might as well let people do what they're going to do anyway."

"Your economic statutes are unlike anything ever attempted. Why will they work?"

John laughed. "Instead of focusing on the negative, look at my ideas. Sure, no one has tried to create an economy with zero business taxes, zero property taxes, zero inheritance taxes, self-regulation, and very low income taxes. But why can't it work? Why do we need high taxes, when low taxes are sufficient?"

"Your economic model relies on income taxes, sales taxes, freeway tolls, and oil and natural gas income for government funding. Is that going to be enough to fund the programs you envision for the impoverished?"

John nodded. "We only have one million people in the county. As long as we can keep the poverty rate and health care costs down, we should be fine. And remember, the constitution does not attempt to create a life of comfort for the impoverished. All it does is provide the bare minimum. This is a constitution based on responsibility and initiative. We will create a level playing field and we will create opportunity for all. But it is up to the people to muster the initiative to take advantage of these opportunities.

"One last point. The constitution has the flexibility to raise taxes. We can increase the income tax rate and the sales tax rate.

We can also tax businesses over a certain threshold of income. I'm sure we will find a good balance, where both the economy and the local populace can thrive. While at the same time maintaining a small government."

"That brings up the question of creating a utopian society," Pam said. "Is that your goal?"

John shook his head. "No, that's not the objective. I do have high hopes that we can create a community that people are proud of, but utopia? No. Not even close. Poverty is unlikely to go away under this model. Remember, this is a highly capitalistic economic model, with very low taxes and regulations. It is designed for people to prosper, but not necessarily everyone."

"You seem confident that your education model will work better than what exists today. Why is that?"

"I know it will work much better, but I don't know if it is the best model. We are going to use a privately operated school system, where students can attend any school of their choice. The schools that thrive will get more money than those that do not. The schools will compete against each other, and students will be forced to learn in order to advance. Instead of putting pressure on the teachers to teach, pressure will be on the students to learn. If a student can't pass the 6th grade exit exam, then they won't make it to the 7th grade. If a student can't pass the 8th grade exit exam, then they won't make it to high school.

"The beauty of this system is that every kid that makes it to high school will not only be literate, but prepared for high school. Currently, only about fifty percent of Kern County high school students can make that claim."

"But you are going to exclude thousands of kids from going to high school," Pam said incredulously.

"Initially, yes. However, once kids and parents realize that we are serious, they will take school more seriously. And teachers will feel obligated to ensure that kids don't fail. Currently there is practically no way to fail. We're going change that."

"If these are private schools, then how are teachers paid?" Pam asked.

"The teachers will be paid based on their ability to teach. There will be no tenure and no guaranteed raises or salary levels. Each private company can decide on the right salary to attract qualified teachers. The main DRB will determine how much money will be paid to educate a single student per year. These decisions will impact how much teachers are paid.

"One final point. The reason this is going to work is because school is going to be free all the way through college. We are going to provide opportunity. And after the students and parents see that we are serious, then they will take advantage of that opportunity."

"I'm sorry, John. But this sounds like pie in the sky fantasy. You're going to educate all of the kids. You're going to lower taxes and make the economy thrive. You're going to take care of the impoverished. You're going eliminate politicians. You're going to keep government small. You're even going to give away free healthcare to the needy!"

John nodded. "Yes, we are going to do all of those things and many more."

Pam laughed. "Excuse me for laughing. This is insane."

"No it's not, Pam," John said seriously. "This is real and this is happening. The only reason it hasn't been done before is because no one has tried. Try to punch holes in my constitution. Tell me one thing that can't work?"

"How are we going to afford healthcare?" she asked skeptically.

"We make doctors and dentists and other healthcare providers servants of the community. We eliminate profit from healthcare and make all healthcare providers non-profit. This restricts pay to the top employee of a non-profit to ten times that of the lowest paid employee. This restricts healthcare costs dramatically. Sure, there will be some doctors who will quit or leave Isabella, but I am sure we will get other doctors and dentists who want live here. If you can make five hundred thousand in income and only have to pay ten percent income tax and no property tax. That's not such a bad deal."

"You're very convincing," Pam said, "but I'm not convinced."

John hesitated. He was frustrated that Pam was holding fast to the notion that the current system was still the answer. He did not want her to see his frustration, so he carefully contemplated what to say next. He realized that although Pam was not interested in secession, many of her readers likely were.

John smiled. "What's the worst thing that could happen? The county is already broke. California is already broke. What more could go wrong. There are no jobs and very little hope. Society is degrading and everyone knows it. This constitution can't make it any worse."

"Anarchy. Civil war. Violence. All of those could happen," Pam said in a threatening tone. "You are opening Pandora's box. This could be a dangerous road to go down. Do you really think California is just going to let us form a new country?"

"Excellent point," John replied, with new respect for Pam. "I'm surprised that you have thought this through. That means you have considered the possibility of this referendum being voted on and passing. Since you brought this up, let's discuss it. If violence, or the threat of violence, does manifest, it will not come from this secession movement, which will be peaceful. It will be perpetrated on us by external forces. Those same forces who have stolen our liberty."

"Oh my," Pam said. "So that's what this constitution is about? You think our freedom has been usurped by government and that we need a new constitution to get our liberty back."

John nodded. "Absolutely. And my words will be proven if there is any threat of violence from external forces, such as the California National Guard. They won't come in to protect our rights, they will come to protect theirs."

"That's a strong accusation, John. You are implying that we have all become vassals of the government."

"Isn't it obvious? There isn't one piece of land in America that is privately owned without property taxes. Nobody, not a single person owns any land in America. It's all owned by government. Every piece of it. Isabella will be the first place in America where citizens own their property free and clear.

"Taxes in California are extremely high. The take-home pay for salaries below fifty thousand dollars is paltry. It's almost impossible to save money for the lower and middle class. Most families are living paycheck to paycheck with zero economic security.

"Everyone is getting sick or obese. The cancer rate is out of control. We have epidemics in autism, asthma, and diabetes. Yet, the government protects the very industries that perpetrate these problems. The government and the pharmaceutical companies are practically in bed with each other. Our food industry could care less about nutrition or harmful ingredients. Now we even have genetically modified food, and the government refuses to protect the citizens from these dangerous foods. Some countries are waking up and banning GMO products, but not in the U.S.

"Our education system was allowed to degrade to the point where half the students are not getting a good education. And everyone looks the other way. Why? Because the government has enough power to keep us all in line. Indeed, we have become vassals. We've lost our freedom. It's time to take it back."

"I don't know about you, John. But I feel free. No one told me what to do today."

"Really?" John asked. "You don't feel manipulated? Coerced into following the current zeitgeist? Of yeah, of course not. You are the zeitgeist. You're the mainstream media that tells us all what to believe. Let me fill you in from outside of your myopic gaze. The average person lives their life manipulated into following the herd. They don't have an inkling of freedom. Instead, they are forced to take any job they can find. They then spend every penny they earn just to get by. They don't have time to ask questions, instead they follow the boob tube and are hypnotized into becoming another statistic. Then your mainstream newspaper helps keep them in that hypnotic trance. There's your zeitgeist in a nutshell."

Pam hesitated, a bit stunned by his rant. "So, you think it's my job to keep the people in a trance? Then why am I here interviewing you?"

John felt embarrassed for going to far. "I'm sorry, I was venting about our current state of affairs. I didn't mean to offend you."

"Apology accepted. I have one last one question. Do you really believe that your constitution can deliver the kind of freedom that you desire?"

"Yes, I do. That's why I created my website, and that's why I'm hoping to get a vote on a referendum for Isabella."

Pam reached down and turned off the recorder. "Wow, that was a powerful interview. I hope they let me print it."

"Me, too," John replied. "If they do, you can come back and we can continue that series you want to write."

Pam smiled. "I'd like that."

Pam rose from her chair and thanked John for his time. She made her way to the front door. John had the feeling that he was a mark, or just another source for one of her columns. He didn't feel like she was there to help his cause unless it fit the paper's agenda. The press had become very cold and calculating, just like society itself.

* * * * *

Two weeks later Pam's story appeared in the *Californian*. It went viral soon after. The AP wire service picked it up and it was reprinted in many newspapers and websites across the country. Then a few days later the cable news networks mentioned the story. John's website was inundated. The number of hits was averaging more than a hundred thousand per day and the posts were in the thousands. No one seemed to be going away. Day after day interest increased.

John's local Meetup group grew from 500 people to 5,000. He wasn't sure where he could hold his next Meetup without paying a large fee for an auditorium. His phone was ringing off the hook from journalists and TV producers looking for an interview. He wanted to do the *Charlie Rose* show, but they hadn't called. He told anyone looking for an interview that if they could get him on the *Charlie Rose* show, he would also do their interview. He turned down all of the offers, except for a national morning show and an interview with the *Los Angeles Times*. Both of these increased traffic on his website, but Charlie Rose's show was the right format for his objective, it would give him credibility and legitimacy. Also, people could watch the archived interview on Youtube later, when they heard about the new constitution. It was perhaps the best marketing tool he could think of to get the referendum passed.

John's patience paid off. After two weeks he received a call from the producer of Charlie's show, and the next day he was on a plane to New York.

* * * * *

"John Randall has done something that has captured the attention of millions of Americans. He has written a new constitution and formed a committee to bring it before the voters of Kern County, California. It is a constitution that is audacious in its scope and grandeur, and radical in its intention. I am pleased to have John Randall at this table for the first time," Charlie began.

"Thanks for having me, Charlie."

"While we only have time today to talk about your new constitution, it should be noted that this isn't your normal area of interest. You have written several books on metaphysical topics over the past twenty-five years."

John grinned. "You can say that re-organizing society is only a temporary hobby of mine and that my true vocation is that of a metaphysical writer and lecturer."

"How did a metaphysical author write a new constitution ?" Charlie asked. "I've read it several times and your ideas are compelling and simplified. In a word, they are inspired."

John hesitated and then laughed. "If I tell the truth, a lot of people are going to change the channel. I would prefer to talk about the constitution, and not how it manifested. I don't mind talking about it, I just don't think the mainstream media is the place to do it."

John knew that if he started talking about how his soul and higher self inspired him to write this constitution, he would be considered crazy. Sometimes you can't tell the truth.

"Fair enough. But before we talk about your new constitution, I have a question about motive. You're objective is to split apart from California and form a new country called Isabella. Named after the only major lake in Kern Country. This idea to create a new country had to have come from a significant motive."

John nodded. "Indeed. I can't deny it. I've always been a closet anarchist. When I was old enough to understand society, I realized something was terribly wrong. For as long as I can remember, I've been frustrated with the policies and direction of America. With my new constitution, I've addressed most of the problems everyone is frustrated with. I've written a document that gives us back our liberty."

"That's interesting. When I read your constitution, I wasn't sure if you were trying to create a utopian society or simply trying to rectify the wrongs that exist today. Which is it?"

"The latter," John replied. "I'm much more focused on fixing problems than creating a utopian society. All this constitution does is offer solutions to problems that exist today. The problems are severe, so the solutions also have to be severe. Many consider these solutions radical, but I consider them elegant, practical, and quite workable."

"Let's talk about some of these solutions. You shrink government to the bone and eliminate politicians, while simultaneously offering shelters to the needy. Then you eliminate property taxes and business taxes, and reduce income taxes to a ten percent flat tax."

John nodded. "Yes, this is all spelled out in the constitution on my website. Anyone can read it. Just Google my name and you'll find it. Let me address your question. Politicians and big government are the problems today. They have stolen our liberty and relegated everyone to following their rules. Government and corporations have the power to dictate how we live our lives. And it's getting worse every day. People have lost the ability to live as they desire. For instance, if you want a quality college education and your parents are not affluent, then you will likely end up with a six figure debt when you graduate. Then you have to drag that anchor around for the next decade or two or three, and you may never find the career you sought. That's just one example of how our freedom has been curtailed.

"So, I eliminate politicians by using paid volunteers. People volunteer to work for the government for one year terms. After they serve for one year, they cannot serve again for five years. We use DRBs, which is an acronym for a decision review board. There is only one main DRB which makes the laws. The citizens can vote to overturn any law that the main DRB approves. Any other DRBs and arbitration panels work in support of the main DRB."

"Your structure is very simplified," Charlie said. "A DRB only has ten people. Is that enough to make laws?"

"Sure, why not. The system is self correcting, because the citizens can change anything they don't like. And the guiding principles for the constitution should prevent a multitude of laws."

"Let me read some of those guiding principles," Charlie said. "One. Liberty to be free without encumbrance. Two. Every human is a respected sovereign being with the same basic human rights. Three. Opportunity for everyone, and no one shall be deprived of education and basic necessities. Four. Service to the community and not self-service to oneself. Five. If a person cries out for help, the community will come to their aid."

Charlie paused and John waited for the next question.

"This sounds like a socialistic state that embraces libertarian ideals," Charlie added.

"That's true to a certain extent," John replied. "However, this constitution aspires to create both a humane society, a fair society, and one where freedom and liberty are guiding principles. It tries to do something that no one thinks is achievable—create a society where people are content, happy, and satisfied. Not just a few, but the whole. This is possible if everyone has access to a quality education, to food and shelter, and if no one can get rich without helping the community get rich."

Charlie held up his hand. "But you're only going to give the poor enough to survive. Your structure has no monetary handouts. Isn't that going to create a lower class that is neglected?"

"I don't think so," John replied. "The housing centers will provide room and board, as well as job training and counseling. It will be austere that is true. But it will be safe and there will be opportunity to leave the centers. And if children are in the centers, they will have the same opportunity for a quality education as those not living in the housing centers. So, while it may appear on the surface that they have a lower standard of living, the indigent won't be stuck like they are today. And they will be one job away from escaping poverty."

"So your goal is to create a safety net for the impoverished, equal opportunity for students and businesses, and a government that is tiny yet effective."

John nodded. "Essentially, although it is a constitution that aspires to greatness. Because businesses are not taxed, they have the potential to become extremely profitable. And because these private businesses are not publicly traded companies, the local employees get the profits and not the shareholders. This should make many employees wealthy and the money should find its way into the community in a number of ways."

"Let's change the subject," Charlie said. "Since your government is so small it does not include a military. How are you going to defend the community from external threats?"

"Three ways. The first will be the local police and the retired police who can work as volunteers. Second, there will be no gun control laws, making it easy for the local population to be armed. And third, we will use private militias. These militias will be our army. We won't have an air force or anti-aircraft defenses. Nor will we have tanks or heavy artillery. But anyone who invades and expects us to cooperate will not have an easy time."

"So your defense basically consists of untrained citizens with small arms?"

John nodded. "That about sums it up."

"With everyone armed, aren't you concerned with potential violence in the community?"

John shook his head. "No, quite the opposite. Good people with opportunity do not commit crimes. They use their guns only in self-defense. I do agree with the argument that guns cause murder. The statistics prove this. In every country without guns you have less murders. Places like Great Britain, Australia, and Japan have very few murders, and very strict gun laws. However, we live in a dangerous country that does not have strict gun laws. Without guns Isabella would be left vulnerable. Also, Kern County is a conservative community. It would not work to outlaw guns."

"John, since we are talking about guns and a dangerous world, your constitution eliminates courtrooms, juries, and judges. How will criminals be sentenced?"

"Justice is one of the guiding principles in the constitution, and something we will take very seriously. We accomplish it with an arbitration system and a small prison system. The arbitration panels consist of volunteers. They will be selected from a pool of candidates made up from local citizens. People will serve one-year terms on the arbitration panels, which will consist of five men and five women. They will be paid a salary set by the DRB."

"You also have banishment in your constitution. How does that work?" Charlie asked.

"There are a number of things that can invoke banishment. The first being illegal immigrants. This is how we currently handle immigration issues, so there is no change here. The second is for dangerous or repetitive criminals. We will give citizens the opportunity to mend their ways, but if they are repeat offenders, they will be taken somewhere and left there. This can be somewhere in America or perhaps a foreign country. For dangerous criminals, we will drop them on remote islands where they have a chance to survive."

"Is that humane, John?"

"It's better than the death penalty."

"Your constitution uses the concept that citizenship is a privilege and not a right, and that if you do not uphold the values of the community you can be banished. You also use a system where citizens can bring grievances against other citizens or businesses."

John nodded. "Isabella's system of justice is highly proactive. If a citizen goes rogue, it's unlikely they will get away with it. This is because everyone can easily file a grievance. Offenders found guilty can incur fines, prison, or banishment. Also, if someone is found guilty by an arbitration panel, they can appeal the ruling twice. Remember, this is a very libertarian constitution, so for a citizen to be found guilty by three arbitrations panels of their peers, it would entail a serious breach of ethical behavior or a broken law."

"I like what you're trying to accomplish," Charlie said. "Equality, fairness, justice, economic vibrancy, liberty, freedom. Your goals are quite ambitious, and you have instituted ideas to address everything in a very coherent manner. I want to believe you have a chance at success, but it seems too ambitious, and I do say, radical."

John nodded. "That's the reaction I expect to get. Anyone who proposes a complete facelift to how we currently organize society should be called a radical. But to paraphrase Einstein, you can't solve a problem with the same ideas that created the problem. We have severe problems and we need revolutionary ideas to solve them. Tweaking the system clearly won't work."

Charlie looked down at his notes. "I want to talk about taxes. How are you going eliminate property taxes and businesses taxes, and then pay for government services and a social safety net?"

"Kern County is blessed with oil. We produce about four hundred and fifty thousand barrels per day. At a profit rate of seventy-five dollars per barrel, that is twelve billion dollars in profit annually. Plus, we annually produce over one hundred billion cubic feet of natural gas. The new constitution allows us to tax natural resources at seventy-five percent. Then you add in the ten percent flat tax on personal income, plus the county sales tax, and you have plenty of revenue. If we're short, there is flexibility in the constitution to increase taxes. We could tax some of the five billion dollars in annual agricultural sales, or the one thousand megawatts of wind power in Tehachapi and Mojave. Kern County has one of the largest wind farms in the nation.

"Also, Charlie, if my projections are correct, I expect tax revenue to increase dramatically as the economy takes off. I would not be surprised to see Isabella with a large account surplus. If everything works out as planned, I expect Isabella to have its own bank, with an abundance of gold reserves to back our currency."

"We have time for one last question," Charlie said. "If this somehow passes, how are you going to make the transition? For instance, anyone who is currently receiving a government pension or public assistance is going to get cut off. How are they going to survive?"

"This is something that the DRB is going to have to decide. I thought about putting it in the constitution, but decided it didn't make sense to include it. Instead we will probably do something like a temporary two-year business tax around five percent. The money generated from this tax can be used for assistance checks during the transition period. I don't want to give money directly as a form of assistance, because I think it creates the wrong incentives and behaviors. But for a temporary transition period, I think it will work."

"I wish we had more time, but we're out. I look forward to having you back at this table very soon."

"Thanks, Charlie. I look forward to it."

CHAPTER FOUR: DOOR TO DOOR

Now that the secession movement was firmly begun in Kern County, it was time to push for a referendum. The unemployment rate was over twenty percent and hope had faded that any sort of economic recovery was on the horizon. There was a large contingent of people ready for change, anything that would improve their lives. It was widely accepted that since the economic collapse—after the U.S. government defaulted on its national debt—a major change was needed to turn things around.

John decided it was time to act. He rented the Fox Theatre in downtown Bakersfield and set up an event for his next Meetup group. It only had a capacity of 1,500 seats, so the committee decided to do a live Internet video feed with audio for those who did not get a seat. After one email announcing the free event, all of the tickets were gone. *The Bakersfield Californian,* ran a story about the event. The local news channels would run stories on the day of the event.

* * * * *

When John walked on stage the full capacity crowd rose to their feet in applause.

"Thank you all for coming. It's a historical night. There are fifteen hundred of you in the audience, and thousands more watching live on the Internet. If you came with a question, hopefully it will be answered. Since there are so many of you, please only ask one question. If you absolutely have to ask more than one that is okay, but the answers might be short.

"The constitution has been updated over the past two months since our last Meetup. I have formed a ten-person committee and we have only made changes if a majority voted yes. Any suggestions made today will be reviewed by the committee for additional changes.

"In addition to me answering questions tonight, I am going to give the microphone to you for the remainder of our time. Anyone who has something to say regarding the constitution can come up and speak for five minutes at a time.

"Before we get started with questions, I have some news to announce. It's time to start collecting signatures to get the referendum on the ballot. I would like all of you, including those watching on the Internet, to volunteer to canvas your neighborhood. The instructions on how to do this are posted on my website. We are going to need signatures from at least twenty five percent of the electorate to get this on the ballot. And even that might not be enough. We are going to have to work extremely hard to get enough signatures.

"Once we get the signatures, if the Board of Supervisors refuses to let us vote on seceding, we will use Plan B to exert pressure. This will entail a whole series of actions we can engage in to make their lives uncomfortable. If we still fail, then we will have to vote them out of office. One way or another, we will get this referendum on the ballot."

Many in the crowded yelled and whistled their approval of this approach.

"Okay, let's get started. Form a line down the right aisle and Julie will hand the person in front a microphone."

Just about all of the questions were similar to what he had been asked at the previous Meetup two months earlier and during John's recent interviews. People wanted to know how the economic model was going work; how the education system; the housing centers; the DRB and arbitration panels would work; how militias would work; how the tax system; the healthcare system would work. They wanted to know the details.

John answered each question with the same confidence that he had conveyed since this movement had gone public. He knew the constitution and how it would impact people. The reaction from the crowd was very positive.

They took a break after John answered questions for two hours. He removed his headset as Julie came to greet him. "The local news has a camera crew outside and they want an interview after we're done."

"You think they would do it now?" John asked.

Julie contemplated. "Sure, why not. They're just waiting for us to finish."

John smiled. "Okay, let's go. Let's go tell them why we're here."

"I only have a few minutes," John said to the TV journalist with the microphone. "Can we make it short?"

John waited for the first question and then like a polished politician ignored it and began telling what the event was about and the need for a referendum. He wanted to use this valuable time to tell people what was happening in Kern County. He laid out his plan in only a couple of minutes. Anyone who watched the local news and heard his interview was likely shocked or excited, but probably not in the middle because John was bringing radical change to the community.

John went back on stage. He waved up the first speaker and handed them a microphone.

"My name is Jim St. Claire. My family has had roots in Bakersfield starting from the eighteen hundreds. I say we should support this new constitution and new country. If we don't do it now, while we still have resources to build on, our opportunity it going to be lost. If we wait too long, nothing is going to get better. There are parts of it that I don't agree with. However, it's worth trying, and I think it has an excellent chance of succeeding. It's time to take back our liberty, our freedom, and our way of life. And if we don't remove the politicians, it's not going happen."

One by one the speakers came up. The majority made similarly positive comments, but several focused on the parts of the constitution they didn't like: lenient drug possession laws, government layoffs, and lost pensions. There was also pushback for forcing the impoverished into housing centers and the removal of any gun laws. Others were concerned about creating a new healthcare and education system that might fail.

After another two hours, John went back on stage.

"I want you to know that this constitution is changeable. If one-third of the citizens sign a petition, then the constitution can be modified with a two-thirds vote of the electorate. The people can decide what they want in their constitution. You have the power to decide.

"Okay, one last order of business and then you can go home. If you want this constitution to be implemented, then I need your help. Go to the website and get the instructions for collecting signatures. Once we have enough support from the community, the Board of Supervisors will have to let us vote on a referendum. Let's make that happen."

Many in the crowd exploded into applause.

"Thank you for coming. Good night."

* * * * *

A month later they had obtained 100,000 signatures, which was more than ten percent of the county population. At this pace they would reach their goal in only a few months. John met with the committee and decided on the strategy they would follow.

The ten committee members had been meeting on the first Friday of each month. They met at the same business conference room, which was donated for this purpose.

"The signatures are piling up," John said. "We need to consider a strategy to get the referendum before the voters."

"We're going to need at least twenty-five percent of the registered voters to get their attention, and that might not be enough," Frank said.

"We're going to need three votes from the Board of Supervisors," Susan added. "Right now I don't think we have any."

"Rallies," Julie said. "We need to have a lot of pep rallies."

"Good idea," John said. "We can march downtown. We can hold rallies at the Board of Supervisor meetings, and then go inside and ask questions."

"We can do a marketing campaign using billboards," Charlie said.

"We can give people signs to put on their lawns that say, 'Let us vote for Isabella!'" Jamie said.

"Excellent, I like that," John said.

"That can also be the theme of the billboards," Jackie said.

"After they allow the referendum, we can change them to say, "Vote Yes for Isabella!" Julie said.

"Okay, I think we have some action items," John said. "We will continue to push signature collections. We will begin holding rallies downtown and perhaps at local parks. We will begin a marketing campaign of billboards and lawn signs. All of this will take organization. Who wants to volunteer to do the billboards?"

"I will," Terry said. "What's the budget?"

"Find out how much it will cost to do five billboards for three months, and let me know. I'm sure that will fit in the budget. We currently have a lot money in our account."

Terry nodded.

"Who wants to have the lawn signs made?" John asked.

"I will," Albert said. "How many do you want?"

"Let's start with ten thousand," John replied. "I'm sure that won't be enough. Let's start small and see what kind of resistance we get from the Board of Supervisors."

Albert nodded. "I'll have the signs made so that you can also bring them to rallies."

"Who wants to get permits for rallies downtown and at local parks?" John asked.

"I'll do it," Frank answered. "I have friends downtown. How many rallies do you want to do?"

John hesitated. "Hmm. How about having one the first Saturday of each month?"

The committee was quiet in contemplation.

"I think we should do one every Saturday," Jackson said. "If we're serious, then let's do this."

"Any objections?" John asked.

No one raised their hand or replied.

"Frank," John said, "get permits for every Saturday for the next three months. Let's march downtown the first Saturday of the month and meet at a park on the other Saturdays."

"We can rent River Walk Park and we won't need permits," Jackie said. "We can rent the entire park for a half day. You can rent it up to four months in advance for a thousand dollars."

"How do you know that?" Julie asked.

"A friend of mine considered renting it for a wedding," Jackie replied.

"Okay," John said. "Frank, since you volunteered. Book the park for the next three months."

Frank nodded.

"No, Frank you get the downtown marching permits. I'll book the park," Jackie said.

Russell raised his hand. "Find out when the next Board of Supervisors meeting is going to take place, and get a rally permit for that night."

"Okay," John said, "I think we have enough action items for one month. We're going to start getting very busy, so perhaps we should start meeting once a week."

"Is that a problem for anyone?" John asked.

"I might miss a few meetings," Jackson said, "but I think it is a good idea."

"Any objections?" John asked. "If we do hold them weekly, they should be short. Less than an hour."

There was silence from the committee members.

"Okay, same time next week. See you all then."

John got up from his chair to officially end the meeting. There was some small talk and then they all made their way outside to their cars to drive home.

* * * * *

The first rally at River Walk Park was on a hot summer day, but that did not prevent people from showing up. It attracted 5,000 people. The only marketing the committee did for the rally was post a banner on John's website and a single advertisement in the *Californian* a few days before the event.

All of the local news trucks were there, which would make the evening news. And of course, the local newspaper would do a story. The idea of holding rallies was brilliant and would capture the imagination of the local community. Over the next few months, the rallies would grow in size every weekend. They would become festivals, with local entrepreneurs setting up booths to sell food, T-shirts, and other items.

The committee decided to keep the rallies short and only two hours long. They used the same format each week, with John speaking and answering questions during the first hour. Then he gave the microphone to the public who could speak their minds for the final hour. They decided to use a kill switch on the microphone in case someone started speaking off-topic or in a non-productive manner. This ended up being a good choice, because some people would rant incoherently or share distasteful monologues. Once the crowd starting booing, Julie was quick with the kill switch.

John walked onto the stage and addressed the crowd. "Welcome everyone to another get together and thank you for coming."

The large crowd applauded and whistled. John was pleased by the big turnout and felt confident that people were behind his proposed new constitution and secession plan.

"Next week we are going to hold the rally in downtown Bakersfield. We are going to march and drop-off our first boxes of signatures. We now have a hundred and fifty thousand signatures. That should get someone's attention!"

John paused and the crowd roared their approval.

"The march will begin at Jastro Park. We will walk down Truxtun Avenue to the Kern County Administration building to drop-off our signatures. We have a permit to march down Truxtun, but we have to stay on Truxtun. It's going to be a large crowd, so it is very important that we march in peaceful manner."

* * * * *

The following week 10,000 people showed up at Jastro Park to march to downtown Bakersfield. The Police had blocked off Truxtun from Jastro to the Administration building and there were several police officers lining the route. The committee led the way, with John pulling a wagon holding three boxes of signatures.

Once they got to Chester Avenue, they saw a large crowd of spectators there to greet them. People were screaming and applauding and some were waving Isabella signs. More spectators lined the streets around the Administration building. The news trucks were filming and capturing history. Although the Administration building was closed, Frank had arranged for someone to be there to receive the collected signatures.

John, Julie, and Frank carried the boxes inside then John spoke to the crowd. It was too noisy for most of the crowd to hear him, but those in front could.

"Today we are one step closer to secession," John began. "If the people want to inspire a vote on the referendum to create a new country, then we deserve one. I will do everything I can to help get this referendum on the ballot. We will not give up easily."

The crowd roared their approval.

John spoke for a few more minutes and they marched back to Jastro Park.

* * * * *

Two weeks later the Board of Supervisors asked for a meeting with John and his committee.

The room was crowded with the ten committee members, five Supervisors, and several of their aides.

Supervisor Marquez, who was at the head of the table and appeared to be their spokesman, asked, "What do you want, Mr. Randall?"

Marquez was an alpha male who dominated a room with his quick mind and forceful personality. He was not someone who could be controlled.

"A referendum vote on our new constitution."

Marquez glared at John. "We can't do that. It's too much change. It's too radical."

"Why are we talking, then?" John replied.

"We wanted to meet and let you know that a vote isn't going to happen," said Marquez stubbornly.

John scanned the room. "If we have to wait and vote all of you out of office, then that is what we will do. But we aren't giving up easily. The United States has already broken up, and it's only a matter of time before more countries are formed. Humboldt County will probably be next. Counties and local communities are choosing to go in a new direction and that is what this constitution provides."

"We like some of your ideas, but they are too extreme for us embrace," said Marquez, still dominating the conversation.

"I only need three of you to embrace it," John replied. "I need three of you to realize what it represents and what it can do for the community. You can be part of history. You can be the decision makers who ushered in a new era of abundance. I have no doubt that Kern Country can thrive under this new constitution. You can either accept this new constitution or continue the malaise that we are mired in. Anyone who thinks we are going to regain a semblance of our economic past is misguided in my opinion. Our rallies are popular because people want something new."

Marquez was silent, as was the rest of the room.

John got up. "I think you know where we stand."

The rest of John's committee rose and began to walk out of the room. John stopped at the door and said, "This isn't over yet."

Before the committee could reply, he turned and walked out.

* * * * *

Over the next few weeks, the rallies continued and the signatures were persistently collected, but the referendum movement needed a boost. Then Humboldt County in Northern California, voted to secede and form a new country. They were the first county to secede in California. This energized the secession movement in Kern County.

The Isabella committee decided to hold a large march and rally in downtown Bakersfield. They advertised it on the radio and TV. They also received free publicity from the local media who were constantly running stories about the local secession movement. From all of this publicity nearly 20,000 people showed up to march and another 5,000 spectators came to watch.

John and the committee led the way down Chester Avenue, with many in the crowd waving signs. The spectators on the sidewalks cheered them on. Police officers were there to block off the streets and make sure the demonstrators behaved.

It was a peaceful march, although the crowd was loud and boisterous. It took them thirty minutes to walk to the Rabobank arena. Steadily the seats began to fill. Once they were filled, the ushers began escorting the overflow crowd outside to a large screen set up.

"Woo-woo!" He exclaimed, pumping his fist into the air. "We made it!"

The crowd exploded in applause, whistles, and cheering.

"We're not giving up until they let us vote!"

John paused to let the crowd cheer and then calm down.

"I want to thank everyone for coming. The first order of business is to get more signatures. If we are going to make this referendum happen, then we need everyone who supports the referendum to sign. If there is anyone in the crowd who has not signed the petition, please sign today. There will be several people in the lobby to take your signature. Also, any of you can volunteer to go door to door in your neighborhood and collect signatures for us. We already have 200,000 signatures, but that isn't enough to convince the Board of Supervisors that you are serious."

The crowd began booing.

"I also ask that you please show up an hour before each Board of Supervisors meeting and voice your displeasure. The dates of each meeting are listed on my website."

The crowd roared their approval of this idea.

John did not ask them to march in front of the homes of each Supervisor, but this had already begun. People on his website were calling for this course of action. It was only a matter of time before the pressure led to a vote.

"Okay, that's enough business talk, let's talk about our future."

The crowd roared.

John pressed his remote and the giant screen displayed the Declaration of the new constitution.

Declaration

We the people of Isabella desire to form an independent country that provides its people a community based on fairness, freedom, integrity, honor, justice, equality, and respect. The community will exist as a united whole that works together in harmony and cooperation. No one person or one group shall infringe upon the rights of others. Government shall remain limited in scope and size, with the citizens in charge of making all of the important decisions.

Once it appeared there were roars of approval from the crowd and prolonged applause.

John waited for the supporters to quiet down and then he said, "When I sat down to write the new constitution I knew what I wanted to include. It was actually quite easy to write. We all know what we want from the society we live in. We all have the expectations that I've listed. This is not new. This declaration uses terms that have more clarity than our present day constitution. Moreover, it is stated in such clear terms that it represents our society's goals."

John used his laser pointer to highlight the next line and read the sentence.

"The community will exist as a united whole that works together in harmony and cooperation. The declaration takes the first sentence, which will not be easy to achieve, and then pushes it further, encompassing the concepts of unity, harmony, and cooperation. As a nation, we have never attempted to create a harmonious society. There was an attempt in the 1960s, but the promise was never fulfilled. But I think it is something we would all like to see. We all want to be able to walk at night without any fear. We all want to be able to trust our fellow man. That can only happen if we instill the values that this declaration represents."

John used his laser pointer to highlight the next line and read the sentence.

"No one person or one group shall infringe upon the rights of others. This sentence reinforces the concept of freedom. Hopefully it will have the effect of limiting the size of government. And if any person or group uses power in a nefarious way, hopefully someone will read the constitution and take action."

John read the next line.

"Government shall remain limited in scope and size, with the citizens in charge of making all of the important decisions. While I try to declare that the government shall remain limited in size and scope, a document cannot guarantee that outcome. But the final stanza is

perhaps the most important part of the constitution: the citizens are in charge of all important decisions. Article one, section four, and amendments nine and eleven in the Bill of Rights, also give power to the citizens for making decisions and implementing laws.

"This constitution clearly lays out a government structure that is run by citizens for citizens, and states that there will be no government bureaucrats. All government workers will volunteer to work for a single year out of five. To serve the country will mean to help your country. All volunteers will be given a task they can take pride in carrying out. And volunteers will be selected based on their skill and experience level. To be selected to volunteer will be an honor."

The giant screen displayed the guiding principles of the new constitution.

Guiding Principles

1. Liberty free of encumbrance.

2. Every human a respected sovereign being with equal basic human rights.

3. Opportunity for everyone, and no one deprived of education and basic necessities.

4. Service to the community and not service to ones self.

5. If a person cries out for help, the community will come to their aid.

6. Crime will not be tolerated.

7. Government kept to a minimal level.

8. Thrive and enjoy life.

9. Reach for your dreams, but you may have to work hard to achieve them.

10. Respect the environment, which includes earth, water, air, and all life forms.

"These principles are to serve as our new ethos. The reasons why they have not yet been achieved today are because of our choices and the embedded power structures that maintain the status quo. These reasons can be overcome. All we have to do is try."

John read the first principle.

"Number one. *Liberty free of encumbrance.* In America today we claim to be a free nation, but we are all enslaved to one entity or another. We are all enslaved to the government, and most of us are enslaved to the company we work for. Then there are financial obligations that make us enslaved to our landlord, bank, or credit card company. Our debts enslave us, because our freedom is based on our ability to afford our lives.

"If you are broke in America, you are not free. And to avoid being broke you are forced to do what the government expects of you and what your employer demands. This is not true freedom. True freedom is doing what you want to do. Of course, this is not easily achievable for everyone. But we can create a society that has much more freedom than exists today.

"No encumbrance is a high ideal, but with that ideal we can create a society with less compulsion to obey the dictates of a large government. Or perhaps give our employer or debtors less hegemony over our lives.

"I want to get government out of our lives and allow people more freedom to make their own choices. I want to make life less about survival and more about thriving. And we can do that."

The crowd roared its approval.

John read the next guideline.

"Number two. *Every human a respected sovereign being with equal basic human rights.* With this principle we state clearly that no discrimination will be permitted. We also agree that fairness and equality be embedded in our community. Bakersfield is known as a very conservative community prone to subtle forms of discrimination. This is something that will be difficult to overcome initially. Many have the perception that people aren't equal, that those who are successful are better people than those who are not. This is something that we will need to work on."

John used his laser pointer to highlight the next guideline and read it.

"Number three. *Opportunity for everyone, and no one deprived of education and basic necessities.* I think this is easily achievable if done correctly. The education system can be fixed, and the constitution has a plan to achieve it. The big change is going to be in our philosophy. Creating a less stratified society is a big shift from how we live today. Many who are affluent will be fearful that this is a new socialistic system that can't work. However, if we create opportunity for all, the poverty rate should shrink rather rapidly.

"Many are afraid that if you guarantee basic necessities people will abuse these handouts and that will create big government. I have designed a constitution that prevents either of these outcomes."

John highlighted the next guideline and read it.

"Number four. *Service to the community and not service to ones self.* This is another philosophy change. Currently we have a constitution focused on individualism, with each person seeking their own happiness. We have seen were this has led us, where we don't know our neighbors and everyone seems to belong to opposing groups.

124

"The new government will consist of paid volunteers who work for one-year terms. Everyone is expected to serve in the government if they are selected. This is similar to our current jury system, which works very well. This guideline also reinforces the concept of equality and fairness.

John used his laser pointer to highlight the next guideline.

"Number five. *If a person cries out for help, the community will come to their aid.* This might seem like a bleeding liberal principle, but it's not. Its purpose is to ensure that people in need will not be neglected. It's not necessarily for people in poverty, but for people with unique situations that need help. This is for situations such as when someone needs money for a medical emergency, or perhaps a funeral. We all have times of need, and this helps create values of private charity in the community. We want people to feel they belong to a greater community. We don't want people to feel alone."

John used read the next guideline.

"Number six. *Crime will not be tolerated.* Currently crime is allowed to proliferate throughout the community. We will bring an end to that. We will use cameras on streets, in parking lots, and businesses, along with facial recognition software. We will collect DNA from all citizens. Criminals won't be able to hide. And trust me, white collar crime will be non-existent."

John highlighted the next guideline.

"Number seven. *Government will be kept to a minimal level.* Benjamin Franklin said, after signing the constitution, that we had a Republic, if we could keep it. He had the insight that human nature might destroy what they created. I'm likewise concerned with government creep. While we can add this guiding principle and hope that future DRBs adhere to it, there is no guarantee that government will remain small."

John read the next guideline.

"Number Eight. *Thrive and enjoy life.* I don't know about you, but I like this one. Currently most of us work too hard to enjoy life. Most of us are spending too much time trying to get through each day, each week, and each month to enjoy life. This guideline envisions a society where people work less, have low stress, and passion for what they do. If it can't be achieved, or if it is lost, then rip up this constitution and start over."

Many in the crowd applauded.

John read the next guideline.

"Number Nine. *Reach for your dreams, but you may have to work hard to achieve them.* Each individual will be given an opportunity to reach for their dreams, but it is up to them to succeed. This was written to give children incentive to work hard in school and in life, and not expect a good life to be handed to them."

"Okay, the last item on this list. Number Ten. *Respect the environment, which includes earth, water, air, and all lifeforms.* This is a philosophy change and one that may be antagonistic toward conservative values. However, we need to protect our country. We don't want to breathe unhealthy air or drink polluted water. It is much easier to maintain our environment today than clean it up later.

"As for life forms, this includes animals, plants, and insects. There are no statutes in the constitution that protects life forms. Currently we only have this guiding principle. And unless the DRB creates a law, we won't have any."

John pressed his remote and the giant screen displayed the Overriding Philosophy of the new constitution.

Overriding Philosophy

We are all neighbors and should treat each other fairly and kindly. We are all equals and should consider the humanity of our actions.

Helping one another should be a priority for everyone.

"The philosophy of our new country is already encompassed in the guiding principles. Here it is reinforced. I especially like the last line. Our priorities should not be for selfish pursuits. How we live and how we play should impact society in a positive manner. Whereas this constitution does not create articles and statutes regarding morality, our overriding philosophy does have a tone of morality. Notice that it uses the word 'should' in the last line. Helping one another and living for one another is a philosophy, not a requirement.

"This philosophy can only work if our community is thriving and successful. If everyone is living quiet lives of desperation, there is no time to help others, or to live for others. Under that scenario, we are spending all of our time surviving and getting through each day.

"This overriding philosophy is based on the concept that the people in the community can care for each other and consider everyone family. That is a very high ideal to reach for, but it is worth trying. If we're going to set up a new system, we might as well aim high."

John paused and the crowd applauded and there were a few whistles.

John pressed his remote and the screen displayed the Business Philosophy of the new constitution.

Business Philosophy

Our goal is sustainability over growth, stability over complexity, quality of life over achievement. While competition is required

in a capitalistic system, conflict and battle
do not have to overshadow our humanity.

"I think our business philosophy is just as important as any other aspect of the constitution. It states clearly that we are going to use a capitalistic system based on competition, but this system does not have to be a battle between businesses. There is room for businesses to coexist and help each other using the overriding philosophy of helping each other and helping the community. They key is how businesses compete.

"Currently business is calculating and driven to make as much profit as possible, without regard to consequence. Today if Wal-Mart shuts down competing stores in the surrounding area that is considered part of doing business. This new philosophy is aimed at sustainability and humanity. Instead of competing in a ruthless approach to profitability and growth, businesses will be recommended to follow the business philosophy of the country. If they take more from the society than they give back, arbitration panels can step in and change their behavior.

"Some people are going to object to a capitalistic system that throttles back a growth orientation. They will say it is against human nature not to be ambitious. However, this constitution does not forbade competition against external businesses. It forbids doing harm to local businesses using rigorous competitive practices. Each business must support and help the community and not just its own selfish ends.

"There are sections in the constitution that reinforce this philosophy by reducing the work week and limiting the salary differences between the highest paid worker to the lowest. There are several statutes in the constitution that throttle back a full-fledged market based system built on the pursuit of growth and profits. I have worked in the corporate world and I understand the weakness of the corporate model and what needs to be reformed. This new constitution will make businesses and workers thrive. There is absolutely no reason for us to have twenty percent unemployment when a new economic system is possible."

John paused and scanned the crowed.

"I'm finished with my presentation. I was going to take some questions, but we only have another hour. I would prefer to give the microphone to some of you. Who wants to speak in front of this huge crowd? Come up to the stage and Julie will give you a microphone. She's standing right there in the front row."

A small line began to form behind Julie.

The first speaker made his way to the stage.

"I just want to say that I am thrilled with this new constitution."

The audience roared their approval.

"I don't have a job and haven't had one in six months. My savings is slowly withering away and I don't see any hope on the horizon. The politicians are spinning their wheels doing nothing of substance, and here we have this beautiful new constitution that solves so many of our problems. More than that, it creates the kind of society we have all dreamed of, where the American Dream is a reality. I don't know about you, but I'm going to do everything I can to make that happen."

The crowd roared again with yells, whistles, and applause.

The next speaker came on stage. "I want to echo what the last speaker stated. Healthcare bills have devastated my family. We lost our house, which I didn't think was possible in America. Who knew that if you got sick and couldn't pay your healthcare bill that they could take your house. I'm not up here to garner any sympathy, my point is that our society is broken and we need to do something to fix it. I'm here to do my part. Thank you."

One by one speakers came to the stage and did something they probably didn't think they had the courage to do: speak in front of 10,000 people.

After the hour was up, the committee led everyone back outside, where another 10,000 people greeted them with roars of approval. The throng marched back down Chester Avenue to the Garces Circle. Spectators lined the route and cheered them on. Many people waved signs that said Vote Yes For Isabella!, Vote Yes For Secession!, or I Want My Referendum!

The event at the Rabobank Arena was televised live over the Internet, and was being recorded for Youtube. At least half of Kern Country would see it. Because of all the publicity that surrounded this event, the referendum would now be hard to stop.

CHAPTER FIVE: TIME TO PREPARE

After the event at Rabobank Arena, it was apparent the referendum was gaining momentum. Demonstrators were taking the initiative and greeting the Board of Supervisors when they left for work in the morning. These demonstrations were organized by the readers of John's blog. The members' home addresses were listed along with the time the demonstrations would begin—usually 7 a.m. to wait for a Board member to leave for work.

They also organized demonstrations at each of the Board of Supervisor meetings, and lately were demonstrating outside the offices of the Board. The pressure was clearly increasing. The local news and national news were covering the story in a big way. *CNN* was becoming a fixture in Bakersfield, covering many of these demonstrations.

The committee met every Friday at their usual location. At tonight's meeting John wanted to find a way to increase pressure on the Board.

He began, "Hello everyone. Thanks for coming. I got a call today from a Hollywood producer who wanted to write me a check for one million dollars to support our effort. We have about four million still in the bank, and this adds another million. I know we wanted to save most of this money to advertise for the referendum vote, and I'm ready to begin doing that."

John scanned the committee members seated around the table. "I would like to run a marketing campaign on radio and TV. I have a friend from high school who owns an advertising company who can do this for us."

"What kind of campaign?" Frank asked.

"We can talk about it," John replied, "but I had a few ideas. I would like to create one to increase signatures for the referendum. We can ask people to visit our website and request a form with a return envelop. And we can tell the people of Kern County how many signatures we already have."

Susan nodded. "I like it. Excellent idea."

"I also want to create a campaign to put more pressure on the Supervisors. We can create an ad that shows that they are blocking the referendum. I'll work with Ron, my advertising friend and he can give us some ideas on how to do this."

"Let's put the Supervisor's photos in the ad with big no votes next to the referendum," Jamie said.

"And then big yes votes for the status quo," Julie added.

"What about the Hispanic vote?" Susan asked.

John said, "The third campaign can be focused on all of the people who only speak Spanish. We can create a commercial for both Spanish radio and TV stating that the new constitution will grant them citizenship. It will also ask them to visit the website to request a petition to sign."

"I can create a Spanish page and a Spanish form they can sign," Russell said.

"With the Spanish speaking community, we can increase our signature total to perhaps three hundred thousand," Terry said.

"I have one final idea," John said. "Let's give the Supervisors an ultimatum. We give them three months to approve the referendum or else we begin holding strikes. We can now influence nearly a quarter of the Kern County population. That's significant political power. We can tell people to stay home from work. We can tell people to boycott certain businesses. We can create a lot of discomfort."

"How do we deliver the ultimatum?" Frank asked.

"Let's use *CNN*," Susan said. "I'm sure they would like an interview."

Everyone smiled.

"Sure, that works for me," John said.

"I have an idea," Albert said. "Before you do the interview, hire a national poll service and find out how many in the county support the referendum. If we are over fifty percent, we can use that in the interview."

Everyone nodded.

"Agreed," John said. "Albert, do you want to hire the polling service, or do you want me to handle it?"

"I got it," Albert replied. "What's the budget limit?"

"If it's more than fifty thousand, then bring the estimate back to the committee next Friday. If it's less, just approve it and we'll write them a check."

"Does anyone have any other ad ideas?" John asked.

"Yeah, I have some ideas," Jamie said. "If the budget allows, we can create several different ads that describe what is in each section of the new constitution. We can display parts of the constitution on the screen, then have a voice explain what that statute or article means."

"I like that," Jackie said. "We can educate the public on the new constitution."

"That kills two birds with one stone," Charlie said. "Not only does it put pressure on the Supervisors, but it supports the vote."

"How many ads should we run describing the constitution?" John asked.

"Let's start with three and we can make more if they are successful," Julie said.

"So, we are going to start with six ads?" John laughed. "That's quite a few. We're going to inundate the public."

"Go big or go home," Jackson said.

Everyone laughed.

* * * * *

Everything hummed along. John did his *CNN* interview and gave the Supervisors their ultimatum. The polling began. The commercials started getting made. The Spanish language website was deployed. The rallies continued every Saturday at River Walk Park. The demonstrators continued to make the Supervisors' lives uncomfortable at their homes and at work.

About a month later the commercials aired on local TV and radio stations. As expected the requests for signature forms was intense. They had to hire two local temps to stuff the envelopes. It wasn't long before they had three hundred thousand signatures. They made another commercial that heralded their achievement of more than one third of the community signing the petition to vote for the referendum. They also included the polling numbers, which showed sixty five percent support.

A few weeks later, the Supervisors requested another meeting with the committee. Several of the committee members thought the Supervisors were going to concede, but John knew the battle was likely not over.

They met with the Supervisors in downtown Bakersfield at their offices. As before, the room was crowded with ten committee members, five Supervisors and several aids. Supervisor Marquez seated at the end of the table began.

"We want to make a deal," he said with a serious tone.

"I didn't come to make a deal," John said. "I came to get approval, and a date for a referendum vote."

Marquez glared back at John. "You have enough votes in this room to get your referendum on the ballot, but California's not going for it. They're not going to let you secede."

The committee was noticeably upset. After all of their work, they still hadn't won. They had beaten the Supervisors, but now there was more antagonism to deal with.

"How can they stop us?" John asked, looking at Marquez.

"They have plans, which they intend to carry out. You didn't think you could just cut off their oil taxes and get away with it?"

"No, but we have contingencies for that," John said.

"You want to go to war over this?" one of the other Supervisors asked.

"Of course not," John replied. "This is going to be a peaceful secession."

"We're getting off topic," Marquez said. "We need to discuss a possible alternative to your constitution."

John put up his hands. "I'll listen, but I didn't come here today to let you rip up our new constitution."

Marquez sighed, recognizing that his argument was likely to fail. "California wants to break up into seven states and form a unified country. California has agreed to allow Humboldt and Isabella to become states with significant independence. But it doesn't want new countries in the north and south that are completely independent—and don't pay taxes."

"You just ripped it up," John replied.

"John, we have an offer for you," Marquez said. "Your committee and our aides can write a new constitution for the State of Isabella. We can keep most of what you have included in your constitution."

John slowly shook his head no. "I understand that creating a new state could benefit the county, but I can't give up on what I know is right."

"John," pleaded the spokesman, "if you don't take this deal, then you get nothing."

"I'll take my chances," John replied.

"Okay, that's settled," one of the Supervisors said. "Let's do an informal vote right now for getting the referendum on the ballot in November."

"Gordon, this isn't the place for that vote," Marquez said.

"Gabe, we both know the outcome of the formal vote. Let's just do it now, so we see where we stand."

Marquez hesitated and then scanned the room. "All in favor?"

Three Supervisors raised their hands, including Gordon.

John let out a long breath. His mind was racing, thinking of the ramifications. "I would like to clear the room, except for my committee and the three Supervisors who just voted yes, along with their aides."

John waited for the others to clear the room. Once the door was closed, he looked at Gordon. "We all know the referendum is likely going to pass. And we also know that the California National Guard is coming to stop us from implementing it. I would like your help in making sure that doesn't happen."

"What do you have in mind?" Gordon asked.

"I know how we can win, but there are few things you can help me with. I would like to meet once a month with you and your aides. Let's team up."

"Sure," Gordon nodded. "You have our support. A new state would have been nice, but I agree with you, it's not the answer. We have to completely start over."

John stood up signaling that the meeting was over. He walked over and shook hands with the three Supervisors who were now on their feet. "Welcome aboard. Let's create a new country."

As John and the committee members walked out of the room, two of the aides handed him their business cards.

* * * * *

A few days later John called one of the aides and setup up a meeting with Gordon. The two of them planned to meet at John's house. Gordon arrived and they sat down for a chat.

John looked at Gordon. "When is the Board going to vote for the referendum?"

"At the next public meeting, which is next week," he replied.

John nodded. "Is there anything that could stop it from happening?"

"As long as myself, Smith, and Thompson show up to vote, it should pass and be placed on the November ballot."

"And California can't stop the vote?"

Gordon shook his head. "No, it's our call. It's a local issue and not part of their jurisdiction."

"But if they're not going to allow the outcome, why won't they come in early and prevent the vote?" John asked.

"It's possible, but not probable," Gordon said. "If they prevent the vote, then they look like the bad guys for not allowing a democratic election that's not in their jurisdiction. However, if they wait until after the election, they can file a lawsuit claiming that the new constitution is unconstitutional. If they win, which is likely, they can say we are breaking the law and call themselves the good guys. They need to spin it so that we have gone rogue and are breaking the law. Then they bring in the soldiers to enforce the law."

"But we are no different than Humboldt," John said.

"This is where it gets tricky," Gordon said. "Humboldt did not write a new constitution. They pretty much left their government structure in place. They didn't do anything that could be considered unconstitutional other than seceding."

"And they don't have any oil," John said.

Gordon laughed. "Exactly."

They both contemplated what was said

"So, what is this grandiose plan you have to defeat the National Guard?" Gordon asked.

"The same method Gandhi used. Peaceful civil disobedience. We've been buying camping supplies for four thousand people to last ninety days. We also have fifteen apartment and house rentals near Jastro park for toilets and showers. We're ready to go.

"We're going to occupy Jastro Park and Beach Park and then march downtown each morning and surround the county buildings during the day. We're going to shutdown the county government."

Gordon contemplated. "I don't see how you are going to win. They're just going to arrest you."

"That's one of the reasons I want your help," John said.

"In what way?" Gordon asked.

"You have influence on how the budget is spent. Try to decrease the Sheriff Department's budget. And do not cooperate with the California National Guard when they arrive. They are going to want you to help arrest us and house us somewhere."

Gordon gave that a thought. "Bakersfield has already cut their police force to the bone. There won't be any funds to baby sit demonstrators every day or house them in a detention center."

John nodded. "Exactly. So, do what you can to keep funds limited."

"I'll do what I can, but you're going to lose."

"We might lose," John replied, "but if enough people join our demonstrations, our voice will get heard."

"You do realize that your plan hurts the people of Kern County more than the California Government? They can wait you out."

John nodded. "I know. It's not a great plan, but it's our only peaceful option."

"You can only win if you put enough pressure on Sacramento, but I don't know how you can do that."

John contemplated. "Me neither at this time, but I'm confident we will think of something before this is over."

Gordon smiled. "The old hope and pray strategy?"

John smiled. "It's the oldest strategy in the book."

They both laughed.

* * * * *

The following week the Board of Supervisors approved the referendum for the November election. The *Bakersfield Californian* newspaper printed the entire new constitution, along with a poll that showed 65% of the county supported it.

The committee was very busy. They met once a week as a group of ten, and then once a month with the three Supervisors and their aides. There was a lot to do and time was running out.

The committee decided to run the ad campaign that displayed sections of the constitution, such as Article III, Section 2, with a voice explaining what the section meant. The ads would run every night during the local TV news broadcasts until the election. They decided to create several more of these ads to make sure citizens were well informed about what the constitution contained.

Now that the referendum was on the ballot it was becoming easy to raise funds. People from all over the country wanted to support the effort. There was a groundswell of support from people who were frustrated with the stagnant and deteriorating economy. A new constitution was something that generated a lot of interest. John's website, was taking in thousands of dollars in donations a day.

The rallies continued at River Walk Park every Saturday. The crowds were large, with at least 5,000 people showing up each week. The format was usually the same. John would talk for about thirty minutes and then turn the microphone over to the citizens who wanted to address the crowd. Julie was always there to organize the effort and had her handy kill switch ready for anyone with an agenda counter to the committee's goal of passing the referendum.

* * * * *

At the next meeting with the Supervisors, the committee received bad news. Gordon opened the meeting.

"You might have noticed there are a few people missing tonight," Gordon said. "Thompson has joined with the other Supervisors to support an alternative secession plan. This does not mean that our referendum is off the ballot. However, there will be two competing secession plans."

"We now have an organized opposition. They are going to try and divide the votes and attempt to prevent passage of our referendum," Frank said.

Gordon nodded. "That's right. Many people want change, but not everyone wants a radical change. They are going after the moderates and those who oppose some ideas in the new constitution. There are a lot of people who still want government to be run by politicians."

"What's in the alternative referendum?" John asked.

"It calls for Kern County to become one of seven future states that form California," Gordon replied.

"Oh, swell," Jamie said. "All they are trying to do is drain away votes."

"What are they calling the new state?" Jackie asked.

"Kern," Gordon replied.

There was silence as everyone considered the ramifications.

"Okay, here's what we do," John said. "We have plenty of money for advertising. Let's create a couple of commercials that attack a new state solution and a couple that focus on the Hispanic vote. Remember we are offering citizenship to everyone who currently lives in Kern County. That gives many voters a strong incentive."

"All we need is fifty-one percent of the vote. We can do it," Julie said.

Everyone nodded their support.

"Gordon, is Thompson a threat to us?" John asked.

Gordon shook his head. "No, I spoke with Thompson, and he is not going to reveal our committee's plans. Also, he said he will support the new constitution if it passed, but would prefer to go the new state route. We shook hands and I trust him."

John looked at one of the aides. "How much does Thompson and his team know about our preparation efforts?"

"Quite a bit," the aide replied. "They know about the farm where we have been bottling water. They have a general idea of how much food we plan to store. They know the names of most of the storage centers we have been using. If they told someone, they could wipe out our supplies."

"Thanks," John replied. "Okay, from now on let's stop adding supplies to those storage centers, and begin using new ones. Let's increase our food storage in case our supplies are appropriated. Buy a truckload of pistachios and almonds from Paramount Farms. Order a truckload of canned food. And load up on dry beans and rice."

"How about some protein bars? I like those," Russell asked.

"Sure," John replied. "Order as many as you want."

John looked at Charlie. "How much water do we have?"

Charlie answered quickly. "We have thousands of five gallon and one gallon plastic bottles. We have been filling them up at a local farm and sending them to storage centers. We're not going to run out."

"Why are we storing all of this food and water?" Susan asked.

"Gordon, I'll let you have the honors," John said.

Gordon looked at Susan. "Because California is not going to let us have a country without a fight. They intend to stop us."

"A fight? You mean guns and bullets?" Jamie looked surprised.

Gordon shook his head. "No, a political fight. They plan to issue a lawsuit contesting the constitutionality of the referendum if it passes. Once the lawsuit is upheld by the California Supreme Court, they will use the California National Guard to make us stand down."

"Which we will not do," John replied. "Instead we will use peaceful civil disobedience to press our agenda forward. We're not going to give up that easily."

"What kind of civil disobedience?" Jamie asked.

"We are going to shut down the county government," John replied. "We will occupy Jastro and Beach Parks with approximately three or four thousand people. During the day we will surround the county buildings in downtown Bakersfield. I expect this to last several months."

"Why didn't you tell us earlier?" Jaime asked.

"I didn't want it to leak," John replied. "The only people who knew were myself, Gordon, Charlie, Russell, and Julie. Now you all know. If this slips out before we begin our occupation, they could block the parks. We don't want that to happen."

"When will we begin the occupation?" Susan asked.

"After we lose the lawsuit," John replied.

Everyone was silent in contemplation.

"Why will we lose the lawsuit?" Jamie asked.

Gordon answered Jamie. "They will claim that Kern County is part of California and legally owned by California, and that we do not have the right to usurp what is theirs. I'm sure the vote will be unanimous by the Supreme Court, because there is no precedent of a county having the right to secede without the pre-approval."

Everyone was silent.

"That's BS," Jackson said. "They just want our taxes. That is what this about: money."

"Okay, this is getting off topic," John said. "Let's stay on point and focus on what we want to achieve. Speculating on legal outcomes is not beneficial. We need keep our eyes on the goal and do what is achievable."

Susan nodded.

Everyone was silent. John was clearly the leader of the committee. If this was a business, then he would have been the CEO.

"Let's call it a night." John said to end the meeting.

* * * * *

The next day John, Charlie, and Russell met with Gordon and his aides. These meetings was to plan for the possible park occupation that could begin after the election. They sat around a table with several notepads and pens.

"I started buying two-way radios with fourteen channels and a six mile range," Russell said.

"Excellent idea," John said. "Buy at least a two hundred. We can use those for organizing demonstrations."

"How are the Internet hotspots coming?" Gordon asked Russell.

"Another week or two and we'll be done," Russell replied. "I'm creating one at each park with ten megabyte download speeds. We're using repeaters to cover both parks."

"Sounds good," John said. "What about generators for power? Do we have enough of those ordered?"

Charlie nodded. "They are already in storage along with two thousand gallons of gasoline."

John was reading from his supply list. "Clothing and shoes. I think we are good for men, but we should get more for the women. Let's have Jamie order some."

Everyone nodded.

"I have a question," Gordon said. "How we are going to get four thousand people to occupy these parks? We can't simply send out an email and expect everyone to show up."

"Why not?" John replied. "I have our email list from my website and my Meetup group. We can tell everyone our plan once the California National Guard arrives."

"It might not work," Gordon replied. "You might get five thousand for the first day of demonstrations, but how many are going stay and occupy the park?"

John laughed. "Gordon, you've been pessimistic about this plan from the beginning. Have faith. It's going to work."

Gordon smiled. "The hope and pray strategy."

"I'm not worried about filling up Jastro," John replied. "but Beach Park has me a bit concerned. It's almost a mile between the parks, and there might not be a desire to be that far away from downtown. It is going to be a two mile walk every day."

Charlie asked, "John, how many people do you think we are going to need to shut down the county government every day?"

"I don't know," John replied, "but five thousand might not be enough."

"People don't have to live in the park to join the demonstrations," Russell said. "They can drive down every day and join us."

Everyone was quiet.

"That would be good if we could get a lot of walk-ups each day," John said.

"How are we going to move the supplies from storage to the parks?" Gordon asked.

"Trucks," Russell said. "We're going to rent several U-Haul trucks. I've made lists of each of the storage units and what they contain. We will put someone in charge of ordering supplies at each park and others in charge of picking them up."

"That brings up an issue," Gordon said. "These supplies are valuable. What's going to stop someone from calling their friends to come and help themselves?"

"Theft?" John asked.

Gordon nodded. "Yeah."

John looked at Russell. "Make sure that you know the people who are sent to get the supplies."

Russell nodded. "I'll be careful."

Everyone was quiet.

"The first couple of days of occupation we won't leave the park," John said. "We'll spend time getting acclimated. We'll set up our tents and build a stage and setup the PA system. We might as well set up a large screen TV and let people watch movies at night."

"Should we have one large tent as the base camp?" Russell asked.

John nodded. "Yeah, let's put a table inside where people can come and ask for supplies or get directions to the nearby bathrooms and showers. We can also put the generators near the base camp where people can recharge their phones and laptops."

John stood up to end the meeting. "Okay guys. That's enough planning for one night."

CHAPTER SIX: THE VOTE

Once both referendums were placed on the November ballot there was a news frenzy. All of the major news networks and cable networks descended on Bakersfield to cover the story. Because of the competing referendums, John had to spend a lot of time in interviews generating support for the new constitution. The polls were pointing to victory, but it was still too close to call. When he received a call from *ABC News* that they wanted to hold a debate between the representatives of both referendums, he quickly agreed.

Diane Sawyer came to moderate the debate between John Randall and Chuck Henson, who was chosen to represent the new state referendum. It was held on the CSUB (California State University Bakersfield) campus in the Doré Theatre. It was the hardest ticket in town to get and sold out quickly. *ABC News* was broadcasting live and more than ten million people were expected to watch during prime time.

Diane was seated at a table in front of the audience, with John and Chuck standing at lecterns on the stage.

"Mr. Randall has won the coin flip and will go first," Diane said.

John said, "Thank you, Diane. And thank you for coming to Bakersfield and moderating this debate. Our community is grateful for your appearance."

The crowd clapped politely.

"I wrote this new constitution because a simple fix won't work. By creating a new state, you don't fix the political problem, you don't fix the education problem, you don't fix the healthcare problem, you don't fix the economic problem, you don't fix the equality, fairness and opportunity problem. The new constitution I'm proposing fixes all of these issues.

"These are not that difficult to fix when there are no entrenched interests defending the status quo. Tonight, I ask Mr. Henson to explain why our constitution can't solve our problems. I'll tell you in advance that he won't, because he can't. Instead, he'll scare you with accusations of layoffs and crime run amok. He probably won't even talk about his referendum because it doesn't solve anything."

The light came on and John stopped.

"Mr. Henson, it's your turn for opening remarks," Diane said.

"Oh, he's going to solve all of our problems?" Chuck said in a mocking tone. "This new constitution is fairy dust, more than that, it's dangerous. Mr. Randall wants to kick out all of the businesses and fire all of the government employees. That's insane. And if we go down this road there is no turning back. We could end up with a society rampant with crime, a ghetto of shelters Mr. Randall wants to build, and a free market system crippled by rules.

"Let's get to the heart of the matter. He wants to rip up the current constitution and our current way of life. If this passes, life as we know it will go away. And what will we get in return? Mr. Randall says taxes are going to be lowered, but in return for what? Fewer policemen? More crime? A political system run by citizens? How can we expect that to work? And a justice system run by citizen arbitrators? Do we really think that is going to work? Mr. Randall wants to regulate the healthcare system to reduce doctors' pay. Why won't our doctors leave? That could make it very difficult to find a doctor in Bakersfield."

The light went on and Chuck stopped.

"You each have a thirty second rebuttal, and then we will begin with questions," Diane said. "Mr. Randall, you go first."

148

"You will notice that the fear attacks have started. Mr. Henson is just warming up. After he gets done, you will have trouble sleeping tonight."

The crowd laughed and John paused.

"Most of his comments don't deserve a rebuttal, but I do want to talk about crime, since he brought it up twice. We all know that crime is on the rise and is creating havoc. Do you really think seceding to create a new state will address our crime problem? This new constitution solves all problems, including crime. I will explain why tonight when I get more time."

John stopped and waited for Chuck's rebuttal.

Mr. Henson said, "If you believe Mr. Randall is going to reduce crime, I have a bridge for sale that's going cheap. The fact is his plan for crime reduction is to be soft on crime by giving everyone three chances to be found innocent. What kind of a system is that?

"You need to be careful believing what he's selling, because it's a fake, it isn't real. Like I said before, he is selling fairy dust. We are all nervous and concerned that society is breaking down, but that is no reason to give up and sell our soul to the devil."

Many in the crowd laughed, not taking Chuck seriously.

"The first question is for you, Mr. Randall," Diane said. "Why should we vote for your new constitution?"

"I could talk for at least an hour to answer that question, but it really comes down to one reason, we need a fresh start. The problems are too entrenched to be left for politicians to solve. Let's take one problem as an example: crime. Does anyone really believe that politicians can solve this problem? I surely don't. However, I solve it with this constitution. I solve it by creating guiding principles that instill equality, fairness, and opportunity. The overriding philosophy is that we are all neighbors and should treat each other fairly and as equals. And that helping each other should be a priority for everyone.

"The guiding principles state that every citizen is to be respected and that no one shall be deprived of education and basic necessities. Moreover, that if a person cries out for help, the community will come to their aide. It is a constitution that brings everyone together, and creates a business system where everyone has opportunities. It's a constitution where the entire community thrives. Simply put, crime will go down because it won't be necessary. If we build a harmonious society, then there will be no need for crime.

"Mr. Henson seems to think this constitution is soft on crime, however one of the guiding principles is that crime will not be tolerated. We will do everything we can to prevent crime and we will investigate crime thoroughly. We will use cameras, facial recognition software, DNA, monetary incentives, whatever it takes to bring criminals to justice. And our new justice system does not have technicalities or loopholes that lawyers can leverage to absolve their clients. If three arbitration panels of your peers find you guilty, you're going to jail or you can even be banished."

The light went on.

"Mr. Henson, your response?" Diane asked.

"Do you believe this drivel? Mr. Randall thinks he is going to create a utopian society to solve the crime problem. That's been tried before and it always fails. And when it does fail, as any rational person recognizes, crime will rise even higher. The democratic system that America invented is the best government ever devised. I can't believe that I actually have to defend it.

"He wants to govern by a committee of unelected leaders who are unaccountable. That's insane. Then he wants to replace our justice system with amateurs. Those are just two major changes from a radical new constitution. And don't get me started on his economic policies that are completely unworkable.

"We have to save this county, and we have to save California. John Randall is a dangerous man, and his constitution is as radical as you can get. It is one hundred and eighty degrees opposed to our current constitution. We are playing with fire here people, and I implore you not to listen to what this snake salesman is selling.

"This is nothing more than charade by a very convincing magician. Mr. Randall has pulled a spell over everyone with his promises of solutions, when in fact he is going to make things much worse than they already have become. He's Harry Houdini come back to life. Only this time he's using the misdirection of replacing our current constitution with one that is made of a fantasy."

Diane smiled at Chuck's theatrics. "Mr. Henson this question is for you. Why do you think creating a new state will be better than the current situation?"

"I'm not sure that it will, but the people of Kern County want to try something different. They are tired of the economic stagnation and stagflation. Unemployment is at extreme levels and taxes are very high. Food and energy prices have been rising beyond the affordability level. We need to do something. I get that. I don't particularly want to form a new state, but we have reached our breaking point. There doesn't seem to be any help on they way, and if we don't try something soon we might not have an economy that can be saved.

"So, while I don't want to form a new state, I don't see any other option to take back some control over our destiny. From my perspective a new state is much more attractive than a radical idea of pulling away from California and going it alone. What happens if we fail. If we form a new state, we know exactly what we are getting and our way of life carries on. This new constitution is whole different animal."

The light came on.

"Mr. Randall, your rebuttal?" Diane asked.

"A vote for a new state is a vote for the status quo. We might be able to lower taxes somewhat, but nearly everything is going to stay the same. Property taxes aren't going to drop or go away. The education system isn't going to improve. Politicians aren't going away. Crime will still be here, and healthcare will still be expensive. To sum up the outcome is easy: the same mess will still be here.

"Let's be honest. The only reason this second referendum is on the ballot is to siphon votes away from the new constitution. If I were in the opposition camp, I would have done the same thing. They don't want a new state. They just want to kill my referendum."

The light went on.

"Mr. Randall, this question is for you," Diane said. "Why are you so confident that this new constitution is going to work?"

John reflected, and scanned the sold out Doré Theatre from behind his lectern. "Because of this crowd. I trust the people. This is my hometown and I know who lives here. I wrote this constitution with very high ideals and high expectations, but I believe in the people to carry it out. We have the mettle, we have the education, we have the values, and we have the knowledge to make it happen. There is nothing in this constitution that is not achievable. It might take some time, but it can work.

"The education system is not going to fix itself in one year, but I think we will be excited at the progress in five years. The same goes for crime and healthcare. I think we can make amazing improvements. As for the economy, I'll tell you straight up that I expect an incredibly vibrant economy that attracts millions of dollars of investment. We will have the lowest corporate tax rate in North America at zero percent, and unions will be outlawed. Get ready for an economic miracle.

"We probably won't have enough local qualified workers for what we are going to need, but people will come. We will experience a building boom, which will boost the entire community. There are going to be too few workers and a very low unemployment rate, likely below three percent."

"Mr. Henson, your rebuttal?" Diane asked.

"There he goes again with his fantasies. Where are these jobs coming from? Just because Mr. Randall is promising to lower tax rates doesn't mean that will solve our economic problems. This constitution is so far beyond the realm of sanity that I find it amazing he is getting any support at all. We should be afraid, very afraid of this referendum passing. A vote for this referendum is a vote for disaster. We're not going to get more jobs. Instead we are going to get chaos."

Chuck stopped, knowing the next question was his.

"Mr. Henson, if you don't want a new state, why are you debating tonight?" Diane asked.

"Well, I would much rather have a new state than lose my hometown to the devil. This constitution legalizes drug possession. That doesn't sit well with me. Do we really think that people are going to be upstanding citizens when so much temptation is legal? Is this really the kind of community we want to have?

"Mr. Randall claims to support a free market system, but he doesn't have any trouble regulating and putting rules on businesses and corporations. When it comes to morality, he considers that hands off. Now why is that? It's simple, he's not a Christian. Did you see the words *In God We Trust* in his constitution? Of course not. Not even the word God is mentioned. Do we really want someone with those values writing our constitution? I don't."

"Mr. Randall, your rebuttal?"

"My religion is not important to this referendum, but since he made this attack, I better defend myself before the media has a feeding frenzy. I consider myself a Christian, although I hold beliefs that are counter to most Christian Religions. I am part of a very small minority of people who *know* that God exists and that we are souls in a human body. In other words, I don't live by faith, but by knowledge or direct knowing of God. This is also called Gnosis, and if you want to categorize me, then call me a Gnostic. But enough about my spirituality. Let's get back on topic.

"America is decaying and needs a new direction. Let's consider the current state of affairs. About one-third of Americans are obese, and about two-thirds are overweight. This has led to an epidemic of diabetes. It has also led to an epidemic of cancer, since weight gain puts an undue burden on the body to retain optimum health.

"The food industry is to blame for much of our weight gain. And a big reason why is that they can sell us nutritionally deficient products. Before we all get sick, you would think the regulators would say *enough*. However, the California FDA is more of an advocate of the food industry than a regulator."

The light came on, but John kept talking.

"Our water is tainted with fluoride, heavy metals, and other chemicals, yet the California EPA looks the other way. Fluoride would be considered toxic waste if we didn't put it in our water. If you look on your toothpaste box it actually gives you a warning not to swallow toothpaste, and to seek medical attention if you do. Why the warning? Because fluoride is toxic. Ironically, they put it in our water. The result is that more than twenty-five percent of children in America have damaged teeth from fluorosis. And babies who are breastfed from mothers who drink fluoridated water are often getting as much as two hundred and fifty percent more fluoride in their systems than babies with mothers who do not drink fluoride.

"It's tragic what is happening today and nothing is being done. My constitution will make water pure and food GMO free."

Diane was listening so intently that she forgot the next question and had to pause.

"Mr. Randall, this is your question. You said a moment ago that your constitution would lower unemployment to three percent and that there would be a shortage of workers. How will that be accomplished?"

John smiled. "I'm glad you asked. Let's begin with the Businesses Philosophy, which prioritizes sustainability over growth. Stability over complexity, and quality of life over achievement. We are going to have a competitive-based capitalistic system. However, the goal is not going to be growth at the expense of quality of life and harmony to the community. Each business will be very close-knit, where the employees share a company's profits equally. This makes the entire community wealthy and not just the top one percent.

"We have specific statutes in the constitution to ensure that the economic system is fair. There are no unions allowed, because they are not needed. The top salary can only be twenty-five times that of the lowest salary for a private company, and ten to one for non-profits. There are no publicly traded companies, so there are no shareholders. Instead of the shareholders getting the profits, the employees share them.

"There are no businesses taxes, unless there is a budget deficit and the DRB deems it necessary. But small businesses can never be taxed, because the first one million dollars of profit is always exempt. Without business taxes, there is no reason businesses can't thrive. Also, with no property taxes, consumers will have more discretionary income to spend, as well as more economic stability and more wealth."

The red light went on, but John kept talking.

"Kern County is unique in that we have an abundance of oil. In fact, it is one of the largest producing counties in the nation.

I estimate that profits are around twelve billion dollars per year at one hundred dollars per barrel.[3] The direct and indirect jobs from oil production create a solid foundation for the economy. All we need to do is build on that foundation to create a vibrant economy. We can tax natural resources and keep seventy-five percent of the profits for the people. This will allow us to have low tax rates.

"And Kern County isn't only blessed with oil. We also have some of the best agricultural land in the country. My grandfather produced three bales of cotton per acre on his ranch. That is about as good as you can get anywhere in the world. Our crops are another foundation we can build on. I also might add that we have one of the largest wind farms in the country to provide us with affordable electricity. There is no reason we can't create a vibrant economy."

"Mr. Henson, your rebuttal?"

"Do you believe this nonsense? Mr. Randall wants to use a communist system of expropriating private property. Our oil fields aren't owned by the people, but he wants to force corporations to sell them at a discount to private companies. What else does he want to do? This is a rabbit hole I don't want to go down. Can we trust him? For all we know, he'll be confiscating farms next for betterment of the community.

"He wants us to believe that our current economic system which uses stocks and bonds is evil and should be banished. Without a stock market, how are we going to invest for our retirement? How are companies going to raise money for IPOs? Do we really believe that banks are going to fund startups? There are so many holes in this plan it looks like Swiss cheese."

A few people in the crowd laughed.

---

3   The production cost is about $25 per barrel in Kern County. At $100 oil, the profit is $75 per barrel. $75 x 365 x 450,000 = $12 billion.

"Mr. Randall wants to eliminate unions. Exactly how is that going to work? What if workers strike and demand a union? Are businesses obligated to refuse to negotiate? And if you eliminate corporate taxes and property taxes, how do you fund the government? It's impossible or else we would have done it already. This whole constitution is a mess. I'm getting tired even talking about it."

Diane smiled. "Mr. Henson, you're going to get your wish. We are now down to final arguments. Mr. Randall, you go first."

"First, I want to correct something Mr. Henson said. He said that the citizens don't own the oil. That's not true. Oil is owned through leases, which are given by the government. These leases are in fact owned by the government and thus indirectly by the citizens. The government has the legal right to determine how these leases are assigned and taxed.

"For my closing arguments, I'm not sure where to begin: education, the economy, or quality of life. They all impact our lives in a huge way. What we do know is that they are all failing us. The quality of our lives has been diminishing. We have rampant crime, high food and energy costs, a health and healthcare crisis, and an economy that is on life support.

"Our education system is broken. Only about half of the students are getting educated. Most of those who are fortunate enough to make it to college end up with significant debt. And our college graduates can't find jobs. Our young people are being deprived of a quality life. They are faced with very few opportunities. Something has to give. We need a new way, a new start.

"My point is that we don't have any discourse to fix our problems. Our corporations and politicians are mired in the status quo, and the populace doesn't have an outlet to express their opinions. They can do it on websites, but those posts seem to die on the vine. I had hope for Youtube, but that hasn't worked either. This is why I gave up waiting for change. I don't see it coming, and I don't think you do either. If you vote for the alternative referendum to form a new state, I don't think that solves anything. We will still have our problems which are continually getting worse. It's time to break away. It's time for a new start. If you haven't read the new constitution please do. It is posted on my website. Just Google my name. Thank you for coming tonight."

The red light was flashing.

Chuck gave his closing remarks and the debate ended. The next day the polls came out with 60 percent supporting the new constitution and only 30 percent supporting the new state, with the rest undecided. The election was only a month away and it was looking good for John's referendum.

* * * * *

The Friday following the debate, the committee met at their usual location. It was amazing that it had remained a secret meeting place all of these months. No one was outside waiting to ask them questions. They were able to meet in relative peace and quiet. This happened because the committee was not known to the public and the press were not following them around.

John had not mentioned the committee in his interviews or public meetings. He felt it wasn't needed and if he could maintain their privacy he would. All he had to do was make sure he wasn't followed to their meetings. Fortunately, Bakersfield was not a large city with a lot of press so no one was following him.

All ten members were present, seated around the table. John initiated the meeting as usual.

"Has anyone noticed or been told about the local TV ads against us?" John asked.

"Yeah, what's going on?" Frank asked. "Someone is running attack ads on every local station."

"I was told it is being financed by the billionaire Koch brothers," John replied. "If you haven't heard of them, they usually back Republican candidates."

"We will need to increase our ad campaign to compete," Susan said.

John nodded. "We can double our budget. We currently have six different ads running. Time is running out, but I'll try to create one last ad that deflects this ad campaign."

"That's a good idea," Jackie said. "This is going to be a close vote with these attack ads running non-stop. We can't underestimate their impact."

"I agree," John said. "We need to be vigilant. I'll create an ad that says these new attack ads are from groups who don't live in Kern County. I'll do some checking, but I'm pretty sure they are coming from outside the county. They are probably coming from the establishment and corporate interests who want to maintain the status quo."

"Excellent idea," Terry said.

"Next point of business is getting out the vote," John said. "We know that at least fifty percent of the people support the referendum, but will they vote? We need to make sure they do."

Julie spoke up. "Our polls show that the only group who opposes the referendum in large numbers is the affluent. If we focus on the middle and lower class, we will have more success."

"I think you have to go door to door," Albert said.

"That's my thought, too," John said.

"Then we need volunteers, and lots of them," Julie said.

Susan raised her hand. "We'll need about a thousand people."

John nodded. "That shouldn't be difficult. Let's do one last large rally to get out the vote and find volunteers. Where should we hold it?"

"I like the Fox Theatre," Jamie said.

Everyone paused in contemplation.

"Yeah, me too," John said. "It's a great place for public speaking. The sound carries well. We can let the public have the stage. It will be a good pep rally."

"And we can televise it live on the Internet," Russell said. "Also, I can create address lists that volunteers can select on our website. I suggest we use lists of two hundred addresses, otherwise people might not be able to get to all of them. I can set up a web page where volunteers can request a list of two hundred addresses? Then once they download the list, it will be no longer be available for anyone else to download?"

Susan nodded. "We need some checks and balances. We don't want to give this list to people who don't use them. So we need to cross-check. We're going to need a list for addresses and another list for follow up phone numbers. Give the phone numbers to people who are currently in the Meetup group. Then have these volunteers do the cross-check to make sure someone knocked on their door."

"That works," John said. "Russell, how long will it take you to setup the web page and collect the address and phone number lists?"

"A week," he replied.

Susan raised her hand. "Russell, can you create a dashboard for each list that shows it has been covered? We don't want to leave anything to chance."

Russell nodded.

"Okay, let's do the rally next Saturday," John said. "That gives us time to rent the Fox and give away tickets on our website. Once we post the event, I would expect the seats to be gone in a few hours. Word will spread very quickly."

"What about the Internet audience?" Jackson said. "Don't we want most of the county to watch?"

"Good point," John said. "*The Bakersfield Californian* has been asking for an interview. I'll do one if they promise to include a plug for the rally."

Julie spoke up. "That will help, but it's not enough. Let's do some radio spots."

John nodded. "Okay. Let's use Chris Connor. He's been doing commercials in Bakersfield for thirty years and everyone knows his voice."

"I have an idea," Jackie said. "We can use all of these volunteers on vote day to do follow up phone calls to make sure everyone voted. We need to rent a hall and get everyone together."

"Excellent idea," John said. "Everyone can use their cell phones. Russell, you can print out the phone lists and we can pass them out."

"After the referendum passes, we can have a celebration party in the hall," Jamie said.

Everyone smiled.

John stood up to end the meeting, and everyone slowly made their way out the door.

* * * * *

Everything was going along as planned. John did his interview with the *Californian*. The new TV ad refuted the attack ad and spun it as coming from outsiders and corporate interests. The radio spots were created to get people to watch the Fox Theatre rally on the Internet. The web page was created to allow volunteers to download address lists and phone lists. The hall was rented for election day for a thousand people.

* * * * *

John stood in front of the crowd on the stage at the Fox Theatre wearing his headset. It was packed full and the crowd was noisy.

"Welcome, welcome! I'm glad you could all come!"

The crowd exploded into applause.

"This is my crowd," John continued. "All of you are part of the referendum Meetup group. Many of you have been supporters from the beginning. Without you this wouldn't be happening."

The crowd roared their approval.

"Well, we have three weeks left. We're ahead in the polls, but it's getting tight and I need you to help us secure victory. I want all of you to volunteer to get out the vote. If you go to my webpage, there is a signup to be a volunteer to get out the vote. You can either go door to door or use your phone to call voters. We will provide addresses and phone lists for you.

"All we are trying to do is make sure that people vote. We are not trying to change their minds. You ask them if they support the referendum. If they say yes, you ask them to vote and tell them their vote counts. That's it. I don't want you to spend time talking about the referendum. Use your time wisely and contact as many voters as you can.

"The first one thousand to volunteer will be part of the election day celebration team. For those in the crowd tonight, you all have the first chance to volunteer. You can sign up in the lobby before you leave tonight. That means that all of you have the opportunity to be part of the victory celebration. For those watching on the Internet, tomorrow morning the website will be open for additional volunteers."

The crowd roared.

"If the people want this referendum to pass, then it will pass. It won't be from a lack of effort."

John paused and waited for the crowd to settle down.

"I'll answer a few questions and then I'm going to turn the microphone over to you. I always enjoy listening to what you have to say. Raise your hand if you have a question and Julie will find you."

Twenty hands shot up immediately. Julie found the person closest to her and handed them a microphone.

A young man in his twenties rose from his seat. "If the referendum passes, how does the transition work? How do we change from our current government to the new government. How do we transfer power?"

John hesitated. "That's a very difficult question. My best answer is that we will figure it out, and that the first couple of years will be a bit messy. There are so many issues to address. For instance, how do you transition into a new school system that is run by private companies? How do you convert to a non-profit healthcare system? How do you convert the salary structures? How do you remove publicly traded companies. The list goes on and on. The transition is going to be very difficult, but we will manage."

John stopped and several hands went up.

Julie found another questioner and handed them a microphone.

It was a middle-aged man, who looked like a successful businessman wearing a nice suite. "John, I don't know about you, but I have a bad feeling that what we are trying to do might not be acceptable to the California Government. Do you think they might try to prevent us from implementing the referendum?"

John hesitated. "These questions are hard tonight. It was much easier when I got questions about the new constitution."

The audience laughed.

"I'm glad you brought this up, because it is a concern of mine. The committee has discussed this and we are indeed concerned. There are even rumors that we could experience a military presence of the California National Guard. In other words, boots on the ground could come to Bakersfield. And if they come, it won't be to help us. But this is a peaceful referendum, and we will never revert to violence in any form. If they come, we will ask them very politely to leave.

"I don't know how many times we will have to ask them, but I plan on implementing this new constitution. I'm not going to give up easily. Do you remember the Occupy Wall Street movement? Well, get ready for the Occupy Downtown movement."

The crowd shouted their approval.

Once John turned over the stage to audience members, the discussion continued on government power run amok. One thing was clear, if California wanted to use force to block the referendum, the people were going to resist to a certain degree. Hopefully everything would remain peaceful.

* * * * *

Three weeks passed and it was vote day. The volunteers had knocked on nearly half of the homes in the county. The first one thousand volunteers, along with the committee and a few other selected people, were at the Bakersfield Event Center making phone calls to get out the vote. The latest poll indicated that they would win. The local press and the national news organizations found out where the referendum headquarters were and were parked outside.

They had catered it with a lot of food. The beer, wine, and champagne would not be delivered unless they won. But it would be quite the victory party if they did.

Once the polls closed, everyone sat around in nervous expectations of victory. There was a large screen TV tuned to the local news that everyone was watching. At 7 p.m. the first results from 25 percent of the counted votes showed the new constitution with 55 percent support, and the new state referendum had 30 percent support. The volunteers cheered their approval, but there was still some apprehension because it wasn't final.

At 8 p.m. and 9 p.m. the support level stayed steady. At 9:30 p.m. the news organizations projected the new constitution referendum would pass. Seventy-five percent of the vote had been counted and the support level held at 55 percent. The crowd was overjoyed at their victory.

Everyone wanted a glass of champagne and a victory speech from John, but he wanted to wait until 90 percent of the vote was counted. So they waited until 11 p.m. Even without alcohol, the crowd celebrated from 9:30 p.m. onward. There was music and people were dancing. A crowd had formed outside and everyone was ebullient.

Once the victory was official, the champagne was poured and party began in earnest. They danced until 2 a.m. John and Julie sat with the committee members and enjoyed the celebration. John had a difficult time feeling elated. He had a nagging feeling that it was not over.

CHAPTER SEVEN: CIVIL DISOBEDIENCE

The morning after the victory John had an interview with Diane Sawyer on *ABC News*. She was his first choice since she came to Bakersfield to hold the debate. Most of the questions had to do with the transition from the current government to the new government in January. There was no talk of resistance from the California Government.

The local paper and national media focused on the victory and there was no mention of a possible problem, but Gordon and the committee were not so naive. They continued to prepare for the worst.

The next day, the President of California came to town and met with the Bakersfield City Council, the County Board of Supervisors, the California Senate Representative and the California Assembly Representatives.

The meeting was held behind closed doors. After the meeting the President held a press conference that all of the meeting members attended, standing behind him. The President stated that the referendum was illegal and would not be implemented until the California Supreme Court ruled on the issue. It was hoped that this ruling could be obtained within three months.

The media asked why Kern County was different from Humboldt. The President had no comment and would not answer any questions.

As John watched the news conference on TV, he knew why: money. He also knew why this was sent to the court. There was no way the high court would allow a county to form a new country without the consent of the political establishment. This gave the President the moral prerogative to be on the right side of the law. John thought it was surreal to see it play out the way he expected. Now we will find out the result, he thought. He had the support of half the county, which numbered nearly a half million people. Of those, perhaps ten percent wanted to protest this decision to call the referendum illegal. That gave him some leverage. Hopefully enough.

Eventually they might lose, but it was too early to give up. And why should they? Society was decaying, and at some point California was going to breakup—one way or another.

John's phone started ringing as the committee members called to get his opinion of the President's decision. He told them this was the beginning and that they would talk at the meeting Friday night.

* * * * *

During the three-month waiting period for the court's decision, planning was in full swing for the expected outcome. Members of John's website and his Meetup group were preparing to protest the final decision by the California Supreme Court. John held two rallies at River Walk Park and said he would implement an Occupy Downtown movement. He told them he would not leave until they were all arrested or everyone gave up. The plan was to hold a peaceful protest asking the California Government to give them their freedom, and the protest could last months.

The additional time waiting for the decision gave them time to buy more supplies. As well as time to plan for an eventual siege. They told their families and friends that the California government was going to win the lawsuit, but that they were going to form an Occupy Downtown movement. Gordon's sources told him that the California National Guard was planning to arrive in Bakersfield shortly after the decision.

In addition to the various storage units being filled, many families and friends were doing their own preparation. Costco had to know something was up, because they were getting inundated with large purchases. Wal-Mart was another source of supplies. Many people were taking trucks out of town, loading up and bringing supplies back.

In December, the committee had their final meeting before the new government was supposed to take effect in January.

Gordon began after everyone was seated. "They're coming. The word I got was five thousand troops will hit the ground on January first. They are going to set up shop on the campus of Cal State Bakersfield and wait for the legal ruling."

"Where did they get five thousand troops?" Frank asked.

"Most of them are ex-military looking for work," Gordon replied. "They will also have armored vehicles and armed helicopters."

"That doesn't matter," John replied. "Our occupy movement will be peaceful. It doesn't matter if the National Guard is armed. We are going to bore them with kindness."

"John, do you think it's time to occupy the parks?" Frank asked. "We could get there ahead of them."

John contemplated. "Sure, why not. Let's move in on New Year's eve."

Julie spoke up. "Let's arrange a rally at Jastro Park and ask everyone to join our Occupy Downtown movement."

John looked at Russell. "Are we ready?"

Russell nodded. "Yeah, I'll rent ten U-Haul trucks. That should be enough."

"It's moving day," Jamie said with a smile. As the meeting ended everyone continued talking to each other as they walked out.

* * * * *

On January 1st, five thousand troops descended on Bakersfield. As Gordon foretold, they setup their base camp on the Cal State Bakersfield campus. Interestingly, they didn't do anything. All they did was setup their tents and get comfortable. The California President didn't even make a public statement.

While the California National Guard was setting up, so was the Occupy Downtown movement at Jastro Park. A thousand small tents were setup in the park the day before. They were ready for the long siege.

A week later the California Supreme Court ruled the referendum unconstitutional with a unanimous vote. The California constitution did not have a statute that allowed secession.

Once the decision was made public, John requested on his website to meet at Jastro Park the following morning at 6 a.m. They were going to hold a peaceful march to downtown Bakersfield where they would hold a peaceful protest at the courthouse and the Kern Country Administration offices. He also informed everyone that his plan was to demonstrate indefinitely, which could take weeks. He asked them to bring a camping pack, along with a sleeping bag. If they didn't have one, there would be packs and tents at the park that they could have for free.

The next morning 10,000 people were at Jastro Park. John led the way, as they marched down Truxtun Avenue to the courthouse. Once they arrived, there were National Guard soldiers and Bakersfield police lining the streets. The demonstrators remained peaceful, although they were boisterous and loud, waving their Isabella signs.

The protestors surrounded the County Courthouse and Administration Building and settled in. They blocked the entrances on Truxtun Avenue and prevented employees from entering. They began their vigil, and had no plans to leave. There were news trucks from the local stations and reporters from the national media.

The National Guard and the Bakersfield Police Department didn't know how to arrest 10,000 people. The protesters sat quietly all day then marched back to the park at 4 p.m.

Some of the reporters came to the park to interview the protestors and find John for a comment. He told them he wasn't going anywhere until they let the citizens of Kern Country have their new country.

The news led to even more protestors the next day. Both parks were literally full, with perhaps 5,000 people. The third day, at 6 a.m. they marched back downtown and repeated the drill. They were peaceful and the National Guard and Bakersfield Police did not arrest anyone.

This continued for about a week and John decided to expand their protests. He setup a large twenty foot by ten foot tent, along with a diesel generator for power. He had a light inside the tent, along with chairs, a table and a laptop computer. This became the makeshift headquarters of the protestors. The committee would meet in the tent and strategize.

"We have an army here in this park," John said to the committee. "Why don't we organize them to expand the protests to other parts of the city. They can go home and take a shower, do a protest and then come back."

"What kind of protests are you thinking of staging?" Frank asked.

"Disrupting transportation," John replied. "We can send in protestors to block roads and freeways. I think we should try to shutdown the entrance to the airport, Interstate 5, and Highway 99."

There was silence as everyone contemplated the ramifications.

"That will just get a lot of people arrested," Jackie said.

John nodded. "I know. It's the price of freedom. We are going to end up with a lot of political prisoners."

There was more silence.

"Everyone agree?" John asked.

Everyone nodded the silent agreement.

John looked at Russell. "Russell, use our email list and send out a daily target for protestors. Hopefully, we can get at least a five hundred people to show up at each target."

"We need someone to lead these protests," Frank said.

"How about you, Frank?" John asked.

Frank contemplated. "Sure, I'm tired of sleeping on the ground."

Everyone laughed.

John looked at Frank. "Try not to get arrested. And make sure to leave once the first few hundred protestors show up. Tell them what to do and then get out of there."

Frank nodded.

"I'll help him," Terry said. "I'll go and watch his back."

John nodded. "Both of you work with Russell, and decide which targets to use. Come and visit us at night and let us know how it goes."

* * * * *

Over the next month the protestors began making progress. Frank and Terry were having success closing down traffic in and out of the County, including the Bakersfield airport. This was creating havoc for commerce. Over a thousand protestors had been arrested, but this only motivated more volunteers. The number of protestors at the park held steady at around 5,000, with some people leaving each day and others showing up.

Both Kern County and Bakersfield had been out of money for a long time. The Bakersfield Police Department and Sheriff's Department were both laying off employees. They did not have the manpower to do their normal duties, let alone babysit the protestors. This led the National Guard to do all of the work themselves. They were spread thin and had a difficult time with Frank's tactics of shutting down roads.

The protestors who were being arrested, were often freed the next day due to overcrowding and a lack of funds for holding them. This infuriated the National Guard who would arrest one of Frank's protestors one day and see them again the next. Once word got out that the protestors where not being held more than a day, more volunteers began to show up. Frank was becoming extremely effective. One day word got out that Interstate 5 was blocked in both directions through Kern Country. Then Frank blocked Highway 99 through Kern County, thereby blocking the normal route through the San Joaquin Valley.

John's protestors became more aggressive, disrupting businesses downtown. After a while, no one was going downtown. He decided to send 3,000 protestors to the state capital, Sacramento to turn up the pressure. In fact, they thought Sacramento was where the protest should be, because it was where the decision makers were located. They would drive up in RVs and march on the Capital Building for a few days with their signs. John invited a few reporters to make sure the story got out. He thought about going with them, but felt his leadership was needed in Bakersfield.

The local and national news trucks were constantly covering both the downtown protests and the road obstructions. When the protestors made it to Sacramento and began a march with their Isabella signs, the media was waiting for them. John and the committee watched it on the Internet from their base camp tent in Jastro Park. The secession movement was having a big impact.

He called Susan in Sacramento. She was the march organizer.

"Susan, I just watched your march on the Internet. It's getting played nationally. You are having a huge effect. Hunker down. You need to keep at this. I think it's going to work."

"A lot of people only planned to stay for a week," Susan replied.

"We'll send you some replacements. Don't worry," John replied. "I'm going to try to get as many people up there as I can."

"That would help," Susan replied. "We are getting a lot of attention, but so far we haven't blocked anyone from going to work."

"I'll get you more bodies," John said.

"You send 'em, I'll use 'em," Susan said with a smile on her face.

"Okay, I gotta go," John said.

"Bye."

The committee members other than Frank, Terry, and Russell, were listening to John on the phone.

"It sound's like it's going well up there," Julie said.

"Indeed," John replied. "We need to get them more protestors. I was thinking why not use people from all over California? Why not invite people who support our cause?"

The committee thought for a moment.

"Oh my god!" Jamie said. "That's brilliant."

"I concur," Jackie said.

"Okay, let's get Russell on this," John said. "He can put out a request on my website and Youtube."

"Hold on," Jackson said. "There's a CNN news truck across the street. Go do an interview."

Everyone looked at John.

"Sure, why not?" John replied as he got up and started walking to the truck.

Twenty minutes later he returned. "That was too easy. They put me on live. I couldn't believe it. I told our supporters to come and help in Sacramento."

Jackson laughed. "They didn't have any time to cut it out."

Everyone laughed.

"Wow," Jamie said. "A lot of people are going to show up."

"We might have enough people to shut down the Capital Building," Albert said.

"I hope so," Jackson said. "That would be great."

"If that happens, we could win," John said.

* * * * *

Over the next few days the number of protestors in Sacramento climbed, as word spread that supporters where needed. The committee only expected people within California to show up, but there were participators from all over America who had already arrived or were on their way.

Within a week, 25,000 people showed up in Sacramento to protest. It had become not just a national news event, but an international event. The committee could not pass up this opportunity to attend. John, Julie, Jamie, and Jackie decided to drive up and join the marchers. They left Charlie, Jackson, and Albert in charge of the base camp tent in Jastro Park.

When they arrived in Sacramento the protestors were boisterous. It was loud and people were waving signs.

There were about twenty California National Guard soldiers in black uniforms carrying automatic weapons, but they were staying clear of the protestors.

John had not shaved in a month or had a haircut. He looked disheveled and in need of a bath, but this only inspired the crowd.

"Hello everyone!" John yelled over a PA system

The crowd roared their approval.

"Thank you for you support!"

More roars from the crowd.

"I just arrived from Bakersfield to join your protest. I left five thousand people at Jastro and Beach Park who have been protesting for a month. We are not giving up until they give us our new country."

More roars from the crowd.

The crowd broke out into a chant of "Isabella, Isabella, Isabella."

John had to wait for the crowd to quiet down.

"I came here to give you message. I want you to surround this building and shut it down. If you can hold it for thirty days that should be enough for our victory."

The crowd roared and then broke out into a chant of "thirty days, thirty days, thirty days."

John waved to the crowed and smiled.

He walked over to Susan and gave her a hug. "We're going back Jastro Park. You stay and finish what you started."

But you just got here," Susan said with a stunned look.

John smiled. "I know. I had to come and make an appearance, but I can't stay. I have five thousand people at Jastro Park who are counting on me to lead. I have to go back."

Susan smiled. "Okay. Thanks for coming, and tell everyone I'm there in spirit."

"I'm going to stay here and help Susan," Jackie said.

"Me, too," Jamie added.

John laughed and looked at Julie. "Are you coming back with me?"

Julie smiled and nodded. "Of course."

"Okay, let's go," John said.

Everyone hugged goodbye and John and Julie walked through the large crowd.

Once they were heading back to Bakersfield, Julie told John her concerns.

"John, with the court ruling how can California allow us to form a new country? How will the politicians in Kern County let us begin a transition?"

John glanced at Julie in the passenger seat. "There is only one way. We have to get the California Legislature to pass a law allowing Kern Country to secede and form their own country. They have to create a law and make Isabella exist."

"Do you really think that's possible?"

John nodded. "I do, otherwise I wouldn't be sleeping in a park."

They both laughed.

"Seriously, John. What are the chances of that happening?"

John thought for a moment. "To be honest, I think it comes down to the will of the people. If enough people demand freedom, the oppressor has to eventually allow it."

"Sometimes that takes generations," Julie replied.

"Let's hope this time we have some form of provident intervention."

"You mean, a miracle?" Julie asked.

"Something like that."

They drove in silence while they both considered a positive outcome.

* * * * *

Two weeks later the referendum protestors got their first break. The Los Angeles basin—composed of more than ten million people and dozens of cities—were experiencing massive riots and looting. Gangs were infiltrating affluent residential areas and conducting home invasions. California had to declare martial law and send in the California National Guard. All of the soldiers in Bakersfield were reassigned to the Los Angeles area. This left the County without any security watching John's protestors.

John had the upper hand he needed. The California Government needed to meet in Sacramento to address the situation in Los Angeles, but the protestors in Sacramento had shutdown the Capital Building. John called Gordon and setup a meeting.

Charlie and John drove to John's house for the meeting. They both showered and it was the first time John had shaved in six weeks.

Gordon arrived with five people, including a California Assemblyman who represented Kern Country.

After formal introductions, the meeting began.

"What would you like to discuss?" The Assemblyman asked.

"I want you to pass a law that allows Kern Country to secede and form a new country called Isabella," John replied.

The Assemblyman hesitated. "You realize if I support you that I am out of a job?"

"Let's negotiate," John said. "I'm sure you have read my new constitution and understand the new government structure. There are two assembly seats and one senate seat that will be lost when Isabella is created. The main DRB is a very powerful committee, and the first DRB will get to influence how Isabella is organized.

"I don't want to make you this offer, but I will if that is the only way to bring Isabella into existence. I'll give the three of you DRB seats. All of you can be on the main DRB."

"That's only one year in office," the Assemblyman replied.

"No, it's for life. You can pass the DRB seat to your family and friends. If you pass it effectively, you can keep a say in the government for years to come."

That Assemblyman contemplated. "I don't know if there is enough support to get this proposed law to pass."

"Sell it like this," John said. "Tell them that it's a win-win vote. They win by getting the government back so they can deal with Los Angeles. And they win by seeing if the Isabella experiment can lead the way to prosperity. Let's face it, you don't seem to have any answers to our problems. Isabella can be an experiment in California's backyard."

The Assemblyman nodded. "Okay, I'll sell it to the others and get back to you." He rose and shook John's hand and headed for the door.

Gordon and the rest of people in the room remained.

"Do you think it will work?" Gordon asked John.

"I hope so," John replied. "I am tired of living in the park." John smiled and everyone laughed.

* * * * *

That night John got a call from Gordon that the Assemblyman wanted the agreement in writing. John suggested they simply include it in the new law they were going to pass.

Two weeks later the California Government decided to cut their losses and focus on saving Los Angeles from anarchy. And if Kern County could show the rest of the country how to prosper, then that might be a good thing.

The new law was passed by both chambers and signed by the President of California. John smiled and gave Julie a long kiss.

"We did it!"

He went outside the base camp tent at Jastro Park and yelled. "We won! Isabella lives!"

The people around the base camp began to cheer and soon everyone heard the news. John thanked all of the supporters in the park, which still numbered over 2,000. It was truly a historic event. The CNN truck was there to capture it live for their national audience. John's short speech would be replayed on CNN and other national media outlets through the day.

CHAPTER EIGHT: ISABELLA IS BORN

The transition was not going to be easy. The first order of business was a transfer of power from the old form of government to the new. Everyone knew John was the leader of the referendum and had to be involved in the transition. John's committee was allowed to negotiate with the various political groups and organizations on how the transition would occur.

The new law stated that the transition could begin immediately. The first thing to do was hold an election for the main DRB. John didn't want to be on the DRB, because he never liked politics, but decided it was a good idea to ensure that Isabella got off to a good start. He wanted Frank to be on the DRB and knew he would be easily elected with John's endorsement.

As written into the law, the three California representatives would be on the main DRB. That meant that along with John and Frank, five more people had a chance to be elected. The committee decided to hold the election in three months, and anyone with a thousand signatures could get on the ballot.

Russell setup a website for the election. All of the candidates were asked to post their résumé and reasons why they would make a good DRB member. The public could then post comments on the candidate's page.

After a couple of weeks, a poll listed the top 20 candidates. These were likely the group of people with the best chance of getting elected. Most of the candidates displayed signs throughout Bakersfield and the county.

John received phone calls every day from candidates seeking his endorsement, but he only endorsed Frank. The committee decided that the first DRB was important enough to require a debate. They organized a debate of the top 20 candidates based on their popularity. The 20 with the most votes on the website were selected. To vote for a candidate you had to become a member of the website, and then you could only vote once.

The top 20 candidates debated live on a local TV channel from the Doré Theatre. The debate was split between two days because they could not all fit on the stage. John was the moderator and asked the questions. Day one, the top ten candidates debated. The process was fascinating and showed incredible passion for the new constitution. Everyone seemed to agree that this new model could work.

On day two, the long shots were given a chance to prove they were worthy. Two of the women captured John's attention. Both were in their mid-thirties and spoke with extreme clarity. He was captivated buy their intelligence and grasp of the issues. He continued to ask them more questions than the other candidates to see if his intuition was correct. They were ideal candidates and what the new country needed. Both were brilliant, personable, and passionate about helping humanity. After he asked the final question and thanked the candidates for coming, he told the audience that this was the first time he had met Elizabeth and Katherine. John endorsed both and told the audience that he hoped they were smart enough to vote for them.

What John didn't tell the audience was that women's influence in the new DRBs and arbitration panels would have a huge impact on how society would be reorganized. Today men are the dominant voice in politics and corporate boards. This would be changing with the new constitution, where half of each DRB and arbitration panel would be women.

On election day, Elizabeth and Katherine both won, along with John and Frank. In addition to this list was a female college professor at Cal State Bakersfield, a successful local businessman whose family had a stellar reputation, and a local city councilman.

The main DRB was given offices and a large meeting room downtown at the County Administration building. It was recognized that the DRB would be reorganizing government and that most of the current city and county employees would be losing their jobs.

When they met for the first time, everyone deferred to John because he wrote the constitution and knew it inside and out.

He had created a project list for the DRB and handed it out to each of the members.

1. Design the Isabella Flag and Seal.

2. Set up a system for hiring government volunteers using one-year contracts.

3. Set up arbitration panels.

4. Set up secondary DRBs.

5. Stop paying taxes to the California Government and adhering to California regulations.

6. Create a citizens database to identify all Isabellans. Create a website for Isabella ID cards.

7. Build centers for both retirees and the impoverished.

8. Set up a method to handle citizen complaints.

9. Begin collecting sales taxes.

10. Award contracts for postal service, garbage, sewer, water, cable, phone service, tolls, prisons, and private schools.

11. Coin money.

12. Set the minimum wage.

13. Implement new wage scale.

14. Convert financial businesses into non-profits.

15. Collect 75% of profit from energy companies.

16. Set the annual government salary structure.

17. Implement 30-hour work week.

18. Implement non-profit healthcare.

19. Implement non-profit multi-housing units.

20. Begin mandatory selling of public companies within one year, to private companies.

21. Implement mandatory selling of residential rentals within on year.

22. Tax farm income over $1 million at 10%.

23. Close fast food restaurants and award contracts to demolish them.

24. Remove GMO products from the shelves of stores.

25. Set up a public voting system.

26. Transition any publicly traded corporations into privately owned businesses.

27. Determine holidays for schools, businesses, and government.

28. Award a contract to design and operate a public transportation system.

John waited for everyone to finish reading.

"I recognize that we want this transition to be as smooth as possible. For that reason, we do not have to rush the implementation of all items. Some we can wait months to implement, and others we can set liberal deadlines for.

"We can also continue using the current government structures until they are no longer needed. We can continue to employ many government workers and we can collect property taxes until the new revenue system is in place.

"We don't have to do all of the work. We can appoint secondary DRBs to help with some of these items. We can also hire government volunteers to be part of our staff. I know all of you have opinions, but let's try not to get bogged down in the details.

"One thing to recognize is that this group has significant power. If anyone in this group has an idea for a law and can get five other members to vote for it, it will become a law. I implore everyone to respect the guidelines in the constitution and not to become overzealous in what you can do. This is a capitalist, libertarian, and humanitarian constitution, and we don't want those ideals to be trampled upon."

Katherine raised her hand. "I have a million questions, but I'll ask the first two that are on my mind. If we each get to name our successor, can we write that person's name down in case of an accident? And if we decide to leave early, will that person get one year on the DRB or only until the end of the DRBs one year session?"

John looked at Katherine. "These are issues that will result in new laws and must be debated in public and then voted on. Currently there is nothing written down to handle either of these situations, but we can easily codify these outcomes."

Katherine nodded. "Perfect. So any details that we would like to codify are okay?"

"Of course," John replied. "We just don't want to spend all of our time writing new laws. We know how that ends up."

"Are we going to televise public debates and voting?" Sebastian asked.

"That's for us to decide," John replied. "I'm in favor of it. We can vote on it during our first public meeting. One thing I would like to do is record our public debate. That way it can be used by future DRBs."

"So, if we have to discuss everything in public, what can we talk about in conference?" Sebastian asked.

"We can discuss anything, but I think we should begin by implementing the new constitution and figuring out how to transition into a new country. All of the items on the list are existing laws we need to implement. For instance, the constitution clearly states that all schools will be run by private companies. All we need to do in public is debate and vote on which private company receives a three-year contract for each school. In conference, we can discuss when we want to do this and how. We can also discuss the merits of each submitted proposal by private companies for awarded contracts. We can even tell each other who we are going to vote for. The important thing is that we award these contracts at a public meeting and that it is done in a transparent manner."

Sebastian nodded. "So we can discuss privately what we think the annual minimum wage will be and then we debate and vote on it in public?"

"Exactly," John replied. "We are the representatives of Isabella, and we each have opinions on what is a fair wage. We don't need to share all of our opinions in public, but we should debate vigorously in conference. That is the only way to get a good law."

"For the minimum wage," Elizabeth asked, "who gets to decide which wage level we vote on first? And is the first yes vote binding?"

"Excellent question," John replied. "I propose we use a lottery system that holds ten balls, and each ball will have our name on it."

Frank laughed. "You mean like the NBA? Where the team names are on the balls?"

John nodded. "Why not. It's simple and it works."

"Let me see if I understand this," Elizabeth said. "For questions that require some kind of order, we are going to use a lottery system with ten balls?"

John nodded. "We can use it for several different things. We can use it for determining the voting order and the debate order. For the minimum wage, whoever is first will get to choose a wage level, and then we will vote on it. If it fails, the second person can choose a wage we can vote on."

"We can also use this same system for awarding contracts," Frank said. "Whoever is first, can name a company for a contract, and then we will vote. This way contracts are awarded fairly."

"Who needs a committee chair when you have lottery balls?" Joe said.

They all laughed.

"Okay," John said, "let's start at the top of this list and work down. Who has some ideas about the flag and seal?"

"What's the seal for?" Gerry asked.

Gerry was the local councilman who won the election. He was a family man and church goer. He was conservative, although moderate on social issues. He had a likable personality which is why he was successful at winning elections.

"It's our country seal for Isabella," John replied. "Every country should have one. It's what we put on our stationary and official documentation. The City of Bakersfield uses their seal on all of their vehicles. You always see the California seal when the President speaks to the public."

"Of course we need one," Mary said. "We need to show off when we do a news conference."

Mary was the college professor. She was petite with very short hair, and wore very conservative clothing. She had a vibrant personality and laughed a lot, but it was mistake to underestimate her intelligence.

Everyone smiled.

"Okay, it's agreed that we will have a country seal," John said.

Mary raised her hand. "Let's hold a citizen contest and they can send their entries to the DRB. Then we can pick the finalists and the public can vote for the winner."

"I like it," John said. "But how many finalists?"

"We will probably get at least a hundred entries," Mary said.

"I have an idea," Joe said. "Any flag or seal that one of us votes for becomes a finalist."

"Let's make it two votes," Gerry said, "to limit the finalists. After all, if only one of us likes it, how good could it be?"

John nodded. "I agree. Two votes is probably better. Anyone else who thinks one vote should be sufficient?"

No one replied.

"Okay," John said. "We need two things to happen. First we need a web page where people can upload their flag and seal designs. I'll take care of that. Russell has already built a website for Isabella.gov. I'll have him design a system where we can vote for as many designs as we like. After the web page is up we need someone to volunteer to tell the public about the contest. Any volunteers?"

"I'll do it," Connie said. She was the former California Assemblywoman.

Connie was Asian and married to a very successful surgeon. She had an aura of someone who was successful and satisfied. She wore expensive clothing and jewelry.

John said, "How long should the contest last? One month?" Everyone nodded in agreement.

Number two. Set up a system for hiring government volunteers using one-year contracts. This includes staffing arbitration panels and secondary DRBs. I think we should use a system similar to the way we create juries. We could randomly select citizens and then question them for their ability to serve. However, we should be methodical, taking several days to decide who the best candidates are."

Mary raised her hand. "I have an idea. We can select a secondary DRB, whose job is to support the main DRB. They carry out whatever we assign them. In this case, they can select another DRB to staff government positions."

"That is a good idea," John said. "We could use a layer of middle management. They can buffer us from the details and allow us to focus on getting this list completed. Does anyone disagree?"

There was silence.

"Okay, let's talk a little bit about the hiring process," John said.

"The volunteers should be required to bring their résumé and a list of references," Mary said.

Gerry raised his hand. "Since the volunteers only need to serve once every five years, they should be able to defer for four years."

"Bring that up in the first public meeting," John said. "We need to codify that."

"If you're going to hire the best people," Joe said, "then you need to use a stringent interview process. I recommend that we invite some of the large companies from Silicon Valley to give us advice. Companies like Apple and Google get a thousand resumes every day. They must have a thorough process we can emulate."

Connie smiled. "Great idea. I'm sure they want us to use their software."

"Any objections?" John asked.

Silence.

"Okay, that's two down and twenty-six to go."

John looked down at his list. "Number three and four we just covered. We will delegate the creation of the arbitration panels to a secondary DRB. Does anyone want to talk about these panels?"

Frank raised he hand. "Are we going to document their processes? For instance, there are a lot of details that go into handling a trial. What are the rules for presenting evidence? What are the rules for deposing witnesses. Do we allow bail? I can think of a list of issues that can get messy."

"This is a good example of the need to go slow," John said. "We don't have to switch to this new system immediately. We can begin with arbitration panels that only handle certain types of cases and then grow from there. As for the rules and procedures, yes I agree they need to be documented. We can delegate this to a DRB."

"I would recommend including some retired judges and lawyers on that DRB," Frank said.

Everyone nodded.

"Number five," John said, "is to stop paying California Government taxes or adhering to California regulations."

"I like that one," Mary said.

"I'll handle this," John said. "All of us should attend the press conference where we announce the flag and seal contests. The dissolution of state taxes can be one of our announcements."

"We can also announce that we will soon be accepting proposals for all of the contracts that we will be awarding," Connie added.

"Who wants that one?" John asked.

"I'll do it," Elizabeth said.

John nodded. "Number six. Create a citizens database. Create a website for Isabella ID cards. This one is kind of tricky because of privacy issues. But it's necessary for immigration control, tracking government service, and public voting. We need to let the public know that it will not be abused and that it will only include their contact and identification information. Which will be their name, phone number, address, eye color, height, weight, photo, and retinal scan.

"This database can be used to cross-reference a government service database, so that we know who to randomly select for government volunteers. It can also be used by employers who can use someone's retinal scan to look them up in the citizen database. If their record is not found, or their photo doesn't match, then they can't be hired."

Gerry raised his hand. "So the database will be public, but you can only access records if you have a retinal scanner. And if I have a retinal scanner on my laptop, then I can look up my information?"

John nodded. "Yes, and you can even update your information and get a new ID card. Anyone in the citizen database can have an ID card mailed to them for free."

"How do people get added to the database?" Frank asked.

"I have an idea," Connie said. "We can setup terminals at post offices and government offices. All you need is a monitor with a camera, a keyboard, and a retinal scanner. We can give everyone a year to get into the system."

"And we can cross-check with the current government database," Mary said. "The state has voter information on most of the citizens. Those who don't create a record in the database can get a follow up letter or phone call. We will need to give a DRB the task of getting everyone in the database."

"Also," John added, "we can use public announcements to let everyone know they need to be in the database to be a citizen. That will create a lot of incentive."

"I'll volunteer to speak about that at the news conference," Katherine said. "I'll let the public know that we will be creating this database soon and that we will need their help."

John smiled. "Thank you, Katherine."

Elizabeth raised her hand. "Since the Isabella Government ID will be needed for traveling on airplanes, a lot of people are going to be motivated to get in the database. Once our California driver's licenses and passports expire, we will not be allowed to travel without a new ID."

"Let's make sure the IDs are impressive looking, perhaps including the country flag," Frank said. "It will give people a source of pride."

"Another contest?" Mary asked.

"Sure, but not by the citizens," John said. "It's just an ID, there is no reason to have the citizens pick the design. Let's have private graphics companies submit proposals. The winner can get the contract for making them for the country."

Everyone nodded.

"Okay, let's do one more item on the list and then we'll break. Number seven. Build centers for both retirees and the impoverished. We are going to need architects and general contractors. Right now many are out of work, so we should get very reasonable proposals. But we need to purchase land to build on.

"These centers are two different things," John added. "The retirement centers will be built to last and can be inside the city limits. We will need these soon because the city and county pensions are going to be cut off. Many retirees will not have enough money to live in their homes.

"We need to build retirement centers with small rooms so that we can accommodate a lot of people in each building. Remember we are not trying to provide a high quality of life. These are centers for people who do not have family who can take care of them ..."

"The healthcare costs are going to be high," Joe interrupted.

"That's a given," John replied. "Our job is to get healthcare costs down to less than ten percent of our GDP. We will have some tough choices, but we can't let healthcare costs impede the quality of life for the entire community."

"Are you saying that we will ration medication and medical treatments?" Mary asked.

"Sure, it could come to that for those in the centers," John said. "It will give people incentive for saving for retirement. We don't want our citizens to rely on being saved by the new government There has to be motivation to save or else people will spend every penny they earn."

The DRB was silent in reflection.

"We will also need centers for veterans and the disabled," Frank said. "They can be designed very similarly to the retirement centers."

"I think they should be more accommodating," Katherine said.

"You mean bigger rooms and more amenities?" Elizabeth asked.

Katherine nodded. "Yes. We don't want them to be too austere."

"This is something that the DRB can decide when selecting the design," John said. "The second type of center is for the impoverished. These will be built outside of the city limits and in areas that are somewhat isolated. They will provide the bare necessities, and will be secured with private security guards. The housing will not be built to last and will be torn down every five or ten years and moved to another location, perhaps a couple miles down the road. The reason for this is that the indigent will not take care of these homes. They will inevitably decay quickly. There will be no cable TV, cell phones, swimming pools, or entertainment. Food will be basic nourishment of soup, bread, fruit, and water. There will be no candy, snacks, soda, or dessert. Supplies will include toothbrushes, toothpaste, shampoo, hand soap, and cleaning supplies. They will be given what they need to survive, but not much else."

"Are these going to be apartment buildings or single family homes?" Gerry asked.

"We can look at the proposals," John replied. "We can probably try both and see what works best. My guess is that we will buy a large farm and start building on it. We could easily need enough housing for ten thousand people initially. But if the economy picks up, that number should start shrinking."

"Will these centers also include schools for the children and job training for the adults," Katherine added.

"The children can take a bus to school, but there will be job training," John said. "They are not built as long-term housing. They are supposed to provide transition housing where people can get back on their feet."

"And don't forget counseling," Elizabeth noted. "A lot of these people just need a little bit of support to turn their lives around."

"I have an idea," Connie said. "We can hire a few government volunteers to work at these centers. They can wear government uniforms so that everyone knows they are volunteers."

"That's a good idea," Mary said. "They can knock on doors and make sure children are attending class or adults have someone to talk to about opportunities."

"Let's be realistic," Gerry said. "Not all of the centers will be safe places to live. Even with security guards, you won't be able to eliminate crime and violence. Anyone who goes door to door will need some security precautions. I would recommend that it is done in pairs. And they should both carry two-way radios to call for emergencies."

"This why we need a two-tier shelter system," John replied. "The first tier is for those who likely will stay less than one year. The second tier is for those who have lived at a center more than a year and look like they are not going anywhere. For these chronic indigent, we should move them to second tier shelters."

"Do you mean that we literally name these centers tier one and tier two?" Mary asked. "And we move people to tier two if they can't find a job within one year?"

John nodded. "We might even want to create a three tiers for the chronically indigent. These are just ideas we can discuss. We can start off with a single tier system and see how it works out. I'm fine with trying that, but my gut says it's not going to work well if we don't create some type of tier system."

There were a lot of nods around the table.

"I have a question that is related to this issue," Gerry said. "What about building codes and building inspectors? That should be something added to our agenda."

"I'll add it to the bottom of the list," John said. "And if anyone else thinks of something we missed, let us know and we will add it to the agenda."

"Sticking to the intent of the constitution, we should form a DRB that creates the building codes," Elizabeth said.

"I agree," Frank said. "They can review all of the existing building codes and come up with a new set. Then we can award private companies contracts to be the country building inspectors."

"That works for me," Gerry said. "If anyone wants to change a code they can file a complaint that can be addressed by an arbitration board."

John smiled to himself. He had created the framework and it was working just as he envisioned. He looked at the clock. "Excellent first session. The clock says it's time for lunch."

Everyone exited the room and headed for lunch.

* * * * *

At their first news conference they announced the flag and seal contest; the cessation of paying California taxes; no longer complying with California regulations; a long list of contract proposals that they would soon begin accepting; and the new citizen database that was mandatory to get a Government ID and become a citizen. They explained what data would go into the database and what it would be used for. They announced that the current government structures would remain in place and would be steadily replaced as new structures were implemented.

It was also announced that the main DRB would meet in front of the public on the first Tuesday of each month, except during vacation weeks and voting months. The public would have the opportunity to ask questions to the DRB members during these sessions. All DRB decisions would be made in public and the new government would be transparent. The public would have the opportunity to overturn laws during voting on the first Tuesday in November, if they could get ten percent of the electorate to sign a petition to overturn a particular law.

The citizens were told that until the DRB made an announcement, nothing in the new constitution would take effect. If an announcement was not made and it was not published on the Isabella.gov website, then the old government system was still in effect. The citizens of Isabella were to be patient during this transition process, which would take more than a year to complete.

* * * * *

The DRB made steady progress over the next few months. Isabella began to take shape. The tax model attracted new businesses. It was the only place in North America with no corporate or property taxes, and a flat income tax of ten percent. It wasn't long before a stream of companies wanted to make Isabella their home. Unemployment dropped dramatically and a building boom took off because of this. The 15 mile Westside Freeway was completed and it looked like suburbia would expand all the way to the Interstate 5. A series of industrial parks were being built along the Westside Freeway to accommodate the influx of new companies.

Just as John had predicted there was a shortage of workers. This didn't last long once word got out. Many were moving to Isabella and filing for blue cards (temporary work permits). The growth rate for new citizens was at 10,000 people per month and increasing. At the current pace of development, it looked like Isabella would double to two million people in a few short years.

The new education system was instigated and looked promising. Isabella had approved the exams for the 6th grade and 8th grade graduation. Students had to score 75 percent to pass. They could go to summer school and attempt to take the test again or else repeat the 6th or 8th grade. High school did not have an exit exam. It was decided that making it to high school and passing all of the required courses was sufficient.

Each school was private and was paid according to the number of students that graduated the year before. They were paid twice a year. In January they received a deposit based on the estimated number of student to graduate. Then in September they were paid the balance based on the actual number of graduates.

Students could attend the school of their choice and switch schools at the beginning of each school year or in January. The teachers were rated by their students (beginning in the fourth grade) and principles were rated by their teachers. These ratings were posted on the Isabella.gov website. Schools were also rated by their students. Each teacher, principle, and school was rated on a scale from 1 to 10 for five different conditions. Averages were then added up into a single rating. These ratings had a big impact on attracting or deterring students.

This rating system also forced principles and teachers to focus on high performance. Students were not allowed to disrupt class, because schools and teachers would be impacted. For this reason, the discipline system was severe. If a student was disrupting the class, then they were removed. School was treated as a privilege and not a right, and if students did not want to attend, they were sent home. There was a second tier school system for students who were not motivated or could not pass graduation exams.

The second tier schools were more lenient, but they would still send disruptive students home. These schools had more than one counselor to help students become motivated. The students who attended tier one schools were given a quality education and were allowed to excel. It was a stimulating learning environment with motivated students and motivated teachers. Every student was given a chance to remain in a tier one school, and many were given a second chance at a tier one school if they attended summer school and showed improvement.

Isabella experimented with different education curriculum. One school embraced a program where the students practically taught themselves. The students picked their own subjects as a group. This method was borrowed from the Anastasia inspired schools in Russia. There were no grade levels or tests. The goal was to learn and enjoy what they were learning. They would select a subject and cover it thoroughly as a group, then move on to the next subject. This method of learning appealed to certain students, who could choose this school. Amazingly, it was discovered that students tended to learn at a much faster rate using this method. Isabella also had an online school for students who preferred to learn from home. And local colleges were almost completely taught online.

Whereas most American cities were experiencing severe budget issues, with many schools closing, Isabella's education system was thriving. This was even taking place among a large proportion of citizens whose first language was Spanish. Isabella decided they would be an English speaking country. For tier one schools, students with English deficiencies were give English homework every night until they were at their grade level. The also had to stay after school for English instruction until they were proficient.

All exit exams were in English, so English proficiency was a requirement in order to make it to the 7th grade and high school. This was practical because high school and college required English proficiency, and all students were told in elementary school that they were expected to graduate from college. A tier one education was a path to college, free to Isabella citizens.

A local movement became very popular with the Isabella citizens, which focused on buying local, eating local, and working local. A webpage was created that listed all of the locally owned businesses, along with posts from people who recommended them. Since the employees of these businesses now benefited from sales, it was beneficial to Isabella to support these local businesses.

Restaurants put up signs of local ingredients that they used. Many purchased local plots where they grew the food they served. When you combined a locally owned restaurant with locally grown food, you had a powerful appeal.

Working for a business that was locally owned was popular and gave you bragging rights. The people of Isabella preferred these businesses, because they knew the money stayed in their community. The theme of *local is better* began to take hold.

The community also became incredibly patriotic, with the Isabella flag flying all over the country. When you combine low taxes with a 30-hour work week, people tend to be very happy. They hung Isabella flags in front of their homes, the ubiquitous flags were everywhere. And if you were an Isabella citizen you had a close kinship with the rest of the community. The constitution had brought everyone together. Even social class couldn't separate the people of Isabella. There was a palpable feeling of community among the citizens. This feeling had extended beyond a neighborhood to the entire country.

There were a few quirks about Isabella. Because of the prohibition of publicly traded companies, it didn't have brand name car dealerships, network television stations, retail chain stores, restaurant chains, or national hotel chains. At first this seemed like a drawback of the new constitution, but soon private companies filled the vacuum. The local television station had a lack of creative programming, but the local news was excellent. They televised local events, especially high school and college sports, which was a boon for the local citizens."

Perhaps the biggest change to the community was its health. Isabella became one of the healthiest places on earth. They had clean water, no fast food chains, a gamut of locally grown organic food, no GMO products, and a focus on eating well. A local doctor had success curing people of diabetes with a plant-based diet. His local TV show was very popular and changed the eating habits of the country. He was handsome and had a magnetic personality. Every week tens of thousands would tune-in and listen to him explain how the body worked and how it reacted to different foods. It wasn't long before everyone was an expert on nutrition.

Another change was that food was no longer wasted by grocery stores and restaurants. Previously, at least 25 percent of all food was wasted mainly due to spoilage at grocery stores and uneaten food at restaurants. Now there was no law that prevented them from giving food away. There was a website listing locations for free food. Local businesses could also list available food and pickup times. A system was set up where trucks would pick up surplus food destined for the trash bin and take it to central locations where people could get it free.

Anyone who wanted a pet dog or cat could go online and look at all of the adoptable dogs and cats in the kennels. There were pictures of the animals along with their approximate age and a short description of their demeanor. All were either spayed or neutered, and had their shots.

The kennels were different than you find anywhere else in the world. The cats were all together outside with small wooden houses they slept in. There was a surrounding fence that had an angled top that could not be climbed by cats. It was called a cat fence and was designed specially to keep cats in your backyard or at shelters. The cats would all play together and there were very few fights. Once in a while they would have to remove an aggressive cat, but trainers could usually change their behavior.

The dogs lived in a series of packs organized by their size. Dog trainers worked with and maintained the packs. Trainers where responsible for keeping the website up to date whenever someone adopted an animal. This was all free, although you could leave a donation when you took a pet home.

Since gasoline prices were high, Isabella transitioned to electric vehicles and public transportation. They created an electric tram system throughout the country that stopped in nearly every neighborhood. The large trams carried more than one hundred people. These were used on the main streets and covered the cities and small towns. These large trams ran on a schedule without a driver and collected electronic payments. The also had various sized trams. These were also self-driving and could be ordered by phone or on the Internet. The smaller trams did not run on a schedule and could be ordered from anyplace in the country. These were essentially a low cost taxi service, whose purpose was to connect you to the main trams.

Once the public transportation system was completed it no longer became necessary to own a car. Those who owned cars used them for convenience and for travel. Previously, the biggest reasons for owning a car were traveling to work and shopping but both of these were solved by the public transportation system and the ability to shop online. After a while, it became quite common to not own a car.

For grocery shopping, consumers could view produce online before making a purchase. Anything they wanted from a grocery store, drug store, or department store was now just a click away. Everything was delivered by a local delivery company who used a fleet of electric trucks. They received a three-year contract from Isabella to do all local deliveries. They kept a database of each customer and reduced costs by collecting packages from different stores and delivering items together. If you ordered an item that came from outside the country, it would be sent to a central location in Isabella and the local delivery company would deliver it to you. This way you could receive your groceries and your shoes at the same time.

It was inevitable that something great would happen to a country this dynamic. Dr. Todd Olson figured out how to extend aging using laser technology. He developed a product dispensed in a liquid spray ingested orally. With three sprays a day not only would you age slower, but it kept you healthy. Isabella's low taxes and low regulations enticed Dr. Todd to move his company to Isabella and market his products to the world.

Isabella eventually qualified to have an Olympic team. They had a track and field athlete who carried the Isabella flag in the opening ceremonies. As Dr. Todd would say, how cool is that?

* * * * *

John and Julie, along with Frank and Jackie continued to get together on weekends. After John and Frank completed their first year on the DRB, they retired from politics. John began a speaking and consulting career, helping other nascent secession movements across North America. Frank and Jackie became his business advisors. Sometimes all three of them would travel together to a speaking or consulting engagement. Julie continued her love of art, working in her gallery. As John would say, they were as happy as a pig in mud.

AFTERWORD

Never before have our lives been more exciting or fulfilling. I can purchase just about anything I want by driving less than 20 minutes, or ordering it on the Internet. Yesterday I bought a Mac Air laptop in less than five minutes and it will arrive in a couple of days via free shipping. If I want to fly to any place in the world, I can order a ticket online with a few keystrokes and credit card number. If I need anything for my house, or food for my kitchen, it is likewise accessible. Stores have no empty shelves. Professionals in every field of expertise are easy to find. I call this way of life "easy street," but as I posited in this book, I don't expect it to last much longer.

Many people today are living a life of ease (as long as they have money in the bank). The degree of abundance for some is quite staggering. We see President Obama living at the White House and going on lavish vacations, and we hardly take notice. He might have a bit more ease than the rest of us, but not much. When his Presidency is over, he will continue to live much the same way, and his nearby neighbors will enjoy the same lifestyle. America has attained such a high standard of living that once we get to certain financial bracket, the degree of comfort can only increase so much more. Sadly, only about 25% of the U.S. Population has achieved this level of material comfort and quality of life. Because the number of those achieving it is no longer increasing, a large chasm between the affluent and the struggling has manifested. We tried to create a nation of opportunity, and it worked for a while. No longer does intelligence and hard work guarantee you a middle class or upper middle class lifestyle.

America is in decline. This began around 1972, the year that middle-class wages peaked. Since then, on an inflation-adjusted basis, the value of a middle class income has dropped. In the 1950s and 1960s, it was quite possible for a family to have a single wage earner. But starting in 1972, that reality began to decline. No longer can a single family wage earner afford life's necessities.

Most of the households in the top 25% of the financial bracket now have two wage earners. Without that second income, they wouldn't have a life of affluence. So, many Americans are working very hard. But just like the hamster on the spinning wheel, they are running as fast as they can just to maintain their way of life.

As a nation this is not sustainable, we are getting tired of our situation. We are not happy with the direction the country has taken. Let's take a look at where we are at in 2014.

* * * * *

I don't want to bury you with facts and charts, but I will give a few pertinent pieces of information. In 1970, energy was cheap and the unemployment rate was low. America was the dominant manufacturer of the world and had a trade surplus. The country had very little debt, and the economy was quite vibrant. Now energy is expensive, and we have stopped making things because of globalization. As a result, our trade and budget deficits have become massive. Our economic problem is slowly strangling us as a nation. No longer do we generate enough wealth to offset our debt. In fact, we are generating more debt than wealth. The only thing preventing an economic collapse is economic manipulation by the Federal Reserve Bank and U.S. Treasury. If the Federal Reserve Bank stopped injecting money into the economy (via electronic money printing), we would be in crisis in a matter of weeks.

The situation is precarious, but the average American doesn't have a clue what is happening. We are in a countdown to a collapse. And nothing—other than a technological invention or perhaps a miracle—can stop it from happening. The Federal Reserve Bank will try to maintain zero interest rates and other stimulus for as long as they can, but at some point a black swan is sure to appear.

There are so many factors impacting the decline of the American Economy that it is hard to pick a place to begin. Let me list ten.

Debt

Debt has exploded for households, corporations, and the government; this has become common knowledge. In 1970, household and corporate debt were both less than 25% of the GDP. Today they are more than 100% of GDP. Thus, it isn't just the government that has become overextended. The average family or business is up to their eyeballs in debt. And the Federal Government by 2020, will have a national debt over $20 trillion. This debt is debilitating because we don't generate enough wealth to service it. Likewise, banks and financial institutions owed an enormous amount of debt are nervous about giving out new loans. This reduces liquidity in the financial markets. It also adds strain to the business environment. Without money flowing into small businesses and corporations, the vibrancy of our economy is limited.

Manufacturing / Globalization

In the 1970s more than 20% of the workforce was employed in manufacturing related jobs. Today that number is below 10%. Instead of recognizing this as a problem, the government exacerbated it by focusing on free trade and globalization from the 1980s onward. If you drive through places like Cleveland, Dayton, and other Ohio cities, they are dreary sites of shuttered manufacturing buildings. There are thousands of these buildings throughout the rust belt, showing evidence of our decline.

Globalization has had the effect of decimating the middle class. Good paying jobs left the country to be replaced by lower paying service jobs. The affluent 25% benefited from this because it led to lower prices for many imported goods from low wage countries. But Globalization was no friend to the vast majority of Americans.

If there are two concepts that will be viewed in history with contempt, the first is globalization and the second is Keynesian economics. I think they are both a scourge. My grandfather would argue it was unions that ruined the country, but they will only make my top ten list. It is ironic that today as I write this, President Obama is on an Asian tour to secure yet another U.S. free trade agreement. His goal, without any trepidation or generating negative press, is to further expand the U.S. globalization agenda. With such naïve goals, (widely accepted by the American public), is it any wonder that practically no one has a clue that a financial collapse is imminent?

Food and Energy Costs

Oil is the lifeblood of the economy, but the era of cheap oil is over. Unless there is a new form of energy discovered, we will be plagued with high energy prices, and they will only go up. While today energy prices are manageable to the average household, they are a drag on the economy. For instance, food equals energy. For every calorie we eat, we need ten calories of energy to produce it. Food prices might be cheap in America, but we will be very lucky if that is true in a few years.

Food prices are going to rise for two reasons (and perhaps three). The first is higher energy prices. The second is inflation from the debasement of the U.S. dollar from money printing. And if those two don't do the trick, there is Mother Nature, who lately has been the bane of farmer's lives. Just ask cattle farmers in Texas and cotton farmers in California, who have both been dealing with extreme droughts.

Food and energy costs are two of the largest costs for the average family and because these are both increasing, consumers have less discretionary income. These rising costs act like a tax on the consumer, and leave them with less money to spend. This has the effect of squeezing other businesses. Already consumers are driving fewer miles to save gas costs, and this trend will continue. Tourism dollars are a big reason why many small businesses exist. Families love to get in their cars and travel and spend money. But this is decreasing.

For those who think the current oil fracking boom is going to be our savior, I don't see that as a likely outcome because we have increased crude oil production in the U.S. from 5 million barrels per day to 8 million since 2010. In order to lower oil prices we would have to do that again, which isn't probable. All this boom has done is buy us time.

Taxes / Regulations

Taxes and regulations are strangling small business, especially in high tax states like California. It has gotten so challenging that small businesses are closing faster than they are opening. The number of small businesses cheating on either taxes, regulations, or both is substantial. They are cheating not because they want to, but because it is the only way to keep their businesses open. The risk level for a small business has risen to the point where you cannot get a loan unless you can secure it 100% with assets. The days of borrowing money based on a business plan are long gone (unless perhaps you can find a venture capitalist).

Government

You may think that the government's impact on the economy is mostly about taxes and regulations, but there is another insidious side. Today government is sucking the life out of the economy by employing millions of people who are ultimately paid by productive businesses through taxation. Approximately 17% of the U.S. workforce is made up of government workers, which requires a huge amount of taxes to pay their salaries and pensions. On top of that are the myriad of businesses supported by government largess. For instance, the multi-billion dollar defense industry is supported by tax-payer dollars. And let's not forget government money given to farmers. When you add up all of the jobs that are paid for by taxpayers, it is probably close to 25% of the economy. The government is by far the largest employer and largest business.

The problem with this is that the government is inefficient and has the power to do what it wants, without adhering to market forces or competition. In effect, the government has grown into a monster. To feed the monster, we have to pay more taxes, thereby making it more difficult for the productive businesses to survive.

Government, just like corporations, only knows how to grow. This growth has turned the government into its own special interest group. The government employs millions of people, both directly and indirectly, and they have to look out for these people's interest and livelihood. Even though millions of people work for the government and not for profit generating businesses, they still expect to be compensated well. This has created an adversarial relationship between government workers and private sectors workers, who pay the salaries of the former.

This was okay as long as there was enough money to go around, but now during the decline of the economy, taxpayers are starting to get a wee bit irritated. This situation will not have a happy ending. The result will be a large number of government workers losing their jobs and pensions. Once the government is broke and can no longer borrow money, taxpayers are not going to be in the mood to pay for an abundance of government workers. Some will be needed, but nowhere near the 17% figure we have today, which doesn't even include the people retired on government pensions or disability.

The number of people receiving government assistance who are supported by private businesses is well over 100 million. Many of these people, I might add, are not means tested and have no need of assistance. The weight of this burden on private business will eventually crush the economy. The government is too focused on keeping the system running to realize it is broken. Meanwhile, the government keeps expanding, expecting to carry on in perpetuity.

I have to mention Obamacare. This abomination of a healthcare law is perhaps the worst piece of legislation to pass in my lifetime. Forcing people to buy something they can't afford is nothing less than autocratic rule. Obamacare is forcing people to buy high deductible healthcare policies that are basically prepaid self-insurance programs. Anyone making less than $50,000 a year can't afford these policies. The middle and lower class is strapped and now they have to come up with $400 a month to pay insurance companies? This monthly payment is buying them the questionable right to pay off a deductible once they need health care. On one plan, if you need a doctor, you pay the $400 monthly payment, and then you get to see the doctor. Whatever he charges you up to the $7,000 deductible, *you* have to pay for. So, you pay $4,800 a year for the right to pay another $7,000 in deductible payments. The insurance company pays everything above $11,800. Who has $11,800 in discretionary income to pay these bills? Welcome to Obamacare.

But it gets worse. Many doctors and hospitals do not accept Obamacare insurance! Why not? They have run the numbers. They know that most people on Obamacare cannot pay the deductibles. The only reason we even have Obamacare is because it is the law. It doesn't seem to bother law makers that is driving up healthcare costs. Many small businesses are being forced to keep only 50 full-time employees because if they exceed that number, they have to offer healthcare insurance. This has the impact of reducing full-time jobs (and increasing part-time jobs). Moreover, because healthcare costs have risen, many employees are being forced to increase their healthcare contributions at work (which are essentially healthcare taxes).

Isn't the outcome to our current economic policies obvious? The private sector is under stress and the government imposes more stress. I'm not sure which will give out first, the U.S. dollar or the private sector.

Corruption

Many would argue that America is not a corrupt country. They would be wrong. The U.S. economy is manipulated by its most powerful citizens. It is tightly controlled by these few with the cards stacked against all others. Approximately 35% of U.S. economic profits this year will go to financial institutions. Another huge chunk will go to pharmaceutical companies. These industries have a negative impact on society because they are not generating wealth for the middle class. They are garnering wealth, but it mostly goes to the top 1%.

The powerful run the country. That would be okay, except they do it for their interests. The rest of us are blocked from effecting a change. If you think this is hyperbole, do an Internet search for how many lobbyists the large corporations have in Washington. If you pull back the covers there are a lot of laws being broken by these powerful corporations who protect their interests and public image by injecting billions of dollars into political elections to garner favor and influence. What is the saying, Money Talks? Well, these corporations have a lot to spend.

Finance and healthcare are only two industries that have the country by the short hairs. The back room deals they make with politicians are only part of the story. There is also the defense industry, the agricultural/food industry, the consumer product behemoths, media, telecommunications, technology, etc. — all of these industries are looking out more for themselves than the country and in many respects, our politicians do everything they can to protect them. That is the only way they can fund their re-elections.

With so much money changing hands in Washington and state houses, it is inevitable that corruption is rampant. This is not blatant law breaking, but a subtle influence undermining the economy. Make no mistake, it is pervasive and ubiquitous in nearly every political domain. And because the top 25% of the citizens are still quite content with their lifestyles, no one with influence is questioning the current state of affairs. Government and corporations work together to conspire against humanity. We have become a nation run by the affluent elite *for* the affluent elite. Little or no influence is being exerted to help solve our pressing problems, or make society a better world for everyone. It's almost laughable how little is being done today, if it wasn't tragic. The number of people coming down with diseases is off the charts, yet this wasn't occurring 50 or 100 years ago. Instead of doing anything about this, we blame it on individual and family choices. In reality, corporations are getting rich from feeding us unhealthy food then treating our illnesses. It doesn't seem to matter how dire the statistics become, we continue to avoid addressing these issues. We avoid them because of one simple reason: those with power block change. If you don't consider that corruption, you need to look a little deeper. If those in power cared about those not in power, we wouldn't be eating GMO food and drinking fluoridated water. Like George Carlin said so eloquently in one of his numerous HBO Specials:[4]

> *"The real owners are the big wealthy business interests that control things and make all the important decisions. Forget the politicians, they're irrelevant. The politicians are put there to give you the idea that you have freedom of choice. You don't. You have no choice. You have owners. They own you. They own everything."*

Demographics

One of the biggest factors limiting the U.S. economy is demographics. Simply put, we are getting too old, and old people don't spend money. We already have everything we need, and tend to stay home. And because America is aging, consumer spending is decreasing. One of my favorite investment analysts, Jeremy Grantham, says that demographics prevent the U.S. from growing at 3%.

When I speak of demographics, I am talking about the aging of the population, and the decrease in the birth rate. These factors create a negative impact on our economic system, which is based on growth. The decrease in the birth rate has been an ongoing phenomenon for several decades and is unlikely to reverse. Without consumers in a consumer-based economy, growth diminishes. It's a numbers game stacked against us. When we are desperate for a 3% growth rate that can pull us out of economic malaise, demographics create an obstacle. Of course, we could create a new economic system that is not so biased toward growth, but that's not a likely outcome.

---

4   http://www.rense.com/general82/carrlin.htm

Education

If our primary education system wasn't broken I would perhaps be optimistic that a solution could be found to our economic problems. Less than 50% of Americans currently enrolled in high school are being truly educated. The rest are being deprived of an education. We tend to blame the students — or their parents — for their failure to achieve. The truth is, most of them never have a chance. Your zip code largely dictates whether you are going to be educated well or not. Again, it's a numbers game. The percentages of students who come from a lower middle class neighborhood have a low probability of getting a good education.

If we have fewer people entering the workforce because of demographics, and the majority of them have a poor education, our economic system will be under strain. How many of them will buy a starter house and be able to fill it with consumer goods? Is it any wonder that the housing market is currently moribund and showing no signs of recovery? We can call ourselves the greatest nation in the world, but our primary education system ranks nowhere near the top. Yes, we do shine in secondary education. This is where the top 25% are given the educational opportunities that the rest are denied. Other countries, such as the rest of the advanced nations of the world, look at us with pity in regards to our educational challenges. Many countries have literacy rates as high as 90%. In America, we would be lucky if 70% could write an intelligent essay. We claim to have a 90% literacy rate, but that's government propaganda. If someone can't write a letter of recommendation for a friend that is legible and lucid, I wouldn't consider that person literate. A literate person is some who can read *and* write. A decline in educational ability is a recent phenomenon. In the 1950s, the quality of education was far superior. Today we put the onus on the students to find their way. In effect, we allow the bright kids to find a way to educate themselves, while the rest are herded along. Those who fall behind are allowed to fail. We make excuses that nothing can be done. It isn't necessarily the teachers who are to blame, but society as a whole, because we all allow this to perpetuate.

I thought President Obama would make it a priority to improve the educational system, but sadly he ignored it. Ironically, it was largely because of his Harvard education that he became President. You would think it would be close to his heart (I'm sure his daughters are getting an excellent education). This goes to show how intractable our problems are when not even a black President can raise the education issue. I'm sure he wanted to, but it is a losing political issue. It's a sad state of affairs. Fixing education would be very simple if we wanted to do it.

Unions

There are a lot of American's who are either members of unions, or support unions and what they represent. However, unions are divisive. A union by definition is created to unite against a common opponent. In most cases, the opponent is management, although lately because of the preponderance of government workers forming unions, the opponent has been taxpayers. Regardless of the employment situation, unions should never be needed. A better solution, one where harmony, integrity, and fairness are the outcome, is what we should strive for.

A country that allows unions is setting itself up for failure because unions will inevitably bleed their opponent dry. This has happened to the ubiquitous manufacturing plants that have closed over the past century and it is happening today, where government workers have leveraged union power to bankrupt cities, counties, and state coffers.

There is a saying that "two wrongs don't make a right." Well, that pretty much sums up unions. Management is wrong to pay workers paltry wages and keep everything for themselves, but creating a union to fix the problem is also wrong. Inevitably it disrupts a business's effectiveness, or taxpayer's ability to pay for 17% of the workforce.

America lost its manufacturing base, largely because of unions. Now the U.S. Economy is hemorrhaging from too much debt, and taxpayers are out of funds. Local, state, and federal governments are trying to squeeze more taxes out of taxpayers, but you can only squeeze so much blood out of a turnip. This need for more tax revenue is wielded by government unions. Police and fireman are paid handsomely and retire in their 50s with high pensions. Those are only two groups of government employees, there are millions of government worker getting fat pensions, when the private sector has pretty much eliminated pensions in favor of 401Ks. This is why so many cities in this country are going bankrupt.

Everyone thought America would grow at a 3% rate indefinitely, and that we could afford early pensions for unionized government workers. It turns out our projections were wrong. Now what? What's coming is bankruptcy on a broad scale. We've already seen it in Detroit, Stockton and a few other cities. The number of cities going broke is significant. Many of the government pensions will not be paid but taxes keep increasing, sucking money out of the private sector to pay for public largess. It's a negative feedback loop, and we all know the outcome.

Illegal Immigration

Illegal immigration has two faces. The first face is positive, this face is the group of hard workers who do jobs no one else wants to do: farm work, restaurant work, meat packing, hotel work, and other jobs that are hard to fill. The second face is not so pretty, this is the group that needs government funds for healthcare, education, food, housing, prisons, and other costs. This second group tends to hold jobs in industries that don't need illegal workers: construction, manufacturing, and blue collar jobs that can easily be filled by Americans.

So, the question arises, what is the cost/benefit analysis of allowing illegal workers access to our country? Is illegal immigration net positive or net negative for the economy? With so many people unemployed and government coffers empty, I think the answer is obvious. If it was net positive, then immigration would be legal and we wouldn't need border control agents.

* * * * *

Life is extremely inequitable today. Fifty million Americans are getting free food from the government because they can barely get by, while 25% live in abundance. This degree of disparity has never occurred before.

Let's call the lower 25% of the economy's citizens the lower class. Many in this group have been subjected to a compulsory education that was extremely lacking. Then they were relegated to finding jobs that could not lift them out of their lower class predicament. A majority of this group live in big cites and are trapped in poverty. Yet they know how people are living on the other side of town — in abundance.

We have created this powder keg. As long as money flows from the government to the lower class, the wick remains dry. But if we go bankrupt and the funds stop, we have a big problem. This group is not going to remain passive. This is why Homeland Security has quietly become a huge internal army. If we have an economic crisis and/or a social crisis, riots will be close behind. The only question is how damaging they will become. Will the riots last one week, or into perpetuity? Will the rioters takeover and destroy some of our cities? The outcome is unknown, but the potential for unrest is there.

This lower class are only part of the problem. The middle class could be even more threatening to the elite because the middle class is the group with resources and leadership skills. This is the group who could form militias and fight back against Homeland Security. They could more easily start a war against the government. Many middle class people are pissed off at government for taking away their rights and their way of life. They have been collecting guns and bullets and are ready to take their country back. I for one, hope this never materializes. One civil war was enough for this country.

While the lower class may only commit robberies and focus on survival in their local communities, the middle class may be revolutionaries with bigger plans. They blame the government for the fall of America and consider government the enemy. They may not hesitate to join a call for rebellion. This creates a very dangerous situation. The irony is we have been spending hundreds of billions of dollars fighting international terrorists, when domestic revolutionaries might be a bigger problem. I feel like getting some popcorn ready to watch how this plays out, because this is going to create a dramatic outcome. We have many different groups all with different agendas vying for different outcomes.

Let's look at a scenario. First, let's assume a financial crisis breaks out and the dollar is abandoned internationally. This could occur if interest rates begin to rise and no one believes that their U.S. Treasury bonds are going to be paid back. If this happens, a negative feedback loop would begin. As more investors and countries dump their U.S. Treasury bonds, interest rates would rise. At a certain point, it would be impossible for the U.S. to borrow money on the international stage. The outcome is that we would be forced to default on our debt.

On that day we would have to cut spending drastically. The first thing to go would be defense spending. The defense budget would drop in half overnight and layoffs would be draconian. Next would be healthcare. We could no longer fund Medicare at 100% or state supported Medicaid programs. This would lead to disastrous layoffs throughout the healthcare industry, with millions of additional layoffs in related businesses.

The Federal Reserve would probably continue to print money in an attempt to stimulate the economy, but the default on U.S. debt would likely be a death-knell for the U.S. Economy. Unemployment would likely rise to 20% very quickly, and even higher.

Under this scenario what do you think will happen to the two groups? Do you think the lower class will stay at home passively while their EBT (Electronic Benefit Transfer) cards are decreased or unfunded? And in addition to less government funds transferring to the lower class, you will have large layoffs that make life very uncomfortable for many. It's going to be a very difficult time.

Then you have the middle class who will have their lifestyles ripped out from under them. This group is likely to be just as angry as the lower class. And the blame will be directed at the government. All we can hope for is restraint and that this period of history is short lived.

Of course not everyone will want to be a revolutionary. There will be millions who adapt to the changes and start a new life. This will lead to many new communities that pop up in new locations.

As you can imagine, under this scenario, secession will be ripe for discussion. There will be many states, cities, and counties that go it alone.

APPENDIX: NEW CONSTITUTION

Declaration

We the people of Isabella desire to form an independent country that provides its people a community based on fairness, freedom, integrity, honor, justice, equality, and respect. The community will exist as a united whole that works together in harmony with cooperation. No one person or one group shall infringe upon the rights of others. Government shall remain limited in scope and size, with the citizens in charge of making all important decisions.

Guiding Principles

1. Liberty to be free without encumbrance.
2. Every human a respected sovereign being with equal basic human rights.
3. Opportunity for everyone, and no one deprived of education and basic necessities.
4. Service to the community and not service to ones self.
5. If a person cries out for help, the community will come to their aid.
6. Crime will not be tolerated.
7. Government kept to a minimal level.
8. Thrive and enjoy life.
9. Reach for your dreams, but you may have to work hard to achieve them.
10. Respect the environment, which includes earth, water, air, and all lifeforms.

Overriding Philosophy

We are all neighbors and should treat each other fairly and kindly. We are all equals and should consider the humanity of our actions. Helping one another should be a priority for everyone.

Business Philosophy

Our goal is sustainability over growth, stability over complexity, quality of life over achievement. While competition is required in a capitalistic system, conflict and battle do not have overshadow our humanity.

Preamble

We hold these truths to be self-evident, that all men are created equal, that they are endowed by their Creator with certain unalienable Rights, that among these are Life, Liberty, Justice and the Sovereignty of the soul. To secure these God-given rights, Governments are instituted among Men, deriving their just powers from the consent of the governed. Whenever any Form of Government becomes destructive of these ends, it is the Right of the People to alter or to abolish it, and to institute a new Government.

Article I

Section 1

The will be no elected officials or politicians. Government employees will serve 1-year terms appointed by decision review boards. Citizens of Isabella will be obligated to serve once every 5 years. They can volunteer for jobs or be assigned. Medical exemptions will be available for the infirm.

Article I

Section 2

Decision review board members will serve 1-year terms and will appoint their replacements. A citizen can only serve on a DRB once every 5 years. Each DRB will consist of 10 members, with 7 members representing a quorum. The number of DRBs necessary for conducting government businesses can be determined by the main DRB. All secondary DRBs shall hold the same level of authority, with the main DRB as the final arbiter.

Article I
Section 3

There shall be no judges or juries. The main DRB will have the authority to assign or delegate to other DRBs, the task of creating 1-year arbitration panels for all disputes, crimes, and misdemeanors. There can be several DRBs and several arbitration panels...whatever the main DRB deems necessary.

Article I
Section 4

The main DRB has the authority to implement new laws, enter into trade agreements, and coin money. However, these laws and agreements can be re-written and changed by the succeeding DRBs. The citizens can vote to overturn these laws by a majority vote. There shall be no citizen voting to implement laws, only to overturn laws. Moreover, laws should be kept to a minimum (refer to Article II). All main DRB decisions will be made at public meetings.

Article I
Section 5

Voting will occur on the 1st Tuesday in November if during the year 10% of the populace signs a petition to overturn a law. Digital signatures and digital voting are both acceptable. All citizens 21 years of age or older are eligible.

Article I
Section 6

All arbitration decisions must be reached within 3 months of the filing. Decisions regarding disputes and crimes can be appealed twice. This can be considered a three strikes process. After three derogatory decisions, it is final. The appeals process must be completed within three years of the first arbitration decision. There is one exception to the three strikes process. If new evidence is discovered, it can be presented to a DRB, which can reinitiate a new arbitration case. If the evidence is compelling, there is no statue of limitations.

Article I
Section 7
DRBs and arbitration panels shall consist of half men and half women. Five of each. A quorum of seven will be needed for making decisions. A majority vote will be used for decisions. Once seven members are present, any DRB or arbitration member will hold stop-work authority if they feel the quorum is insufficient. The DRB and arbitration panel members shall not use their religious beliefs for making government decisions. Instead they will use the principles set forth in the constitution.

Article II
Section 1
Citizenship is a privilege and not a right. Each citizen is responsible for themselves and must hold the values of the community. While each citizen will be respected as a sovereign soul, this does not give them the right to disturb the harmony of the community.

Article II
Section 2
Instead of utilizing a series of laws, the community will rely on a single framework of what is unacceptable behavior. This

will be called Disturbing the Harmony of the Community. This catch-all legal requirement will be implemented by the DRBs and arbitration panels. While this may seem counter to the community's credo of fairness, arbitration panels will ensure it is not abused. The guiding principles of the community shall not be infringed.

Article II

Section 3

No standing army will exist or be organized. Local militias are allowed to form of their own accord, as long as their objective is for the defense and well being of the community. The only permanent government employees will be police and firefighters. Anyone suspected of violating a law or Disturbing the Harmony of the Community can be reported to the police who will inform the arbitration panels

Article II

Section 4

All citizens will be identified as citizens in the government database. This database will include their picture, retinal scan, address, phone number, email, height, weight, and eye color. The government will issue ID cards based on this information, which will be easy to obtain. The data should be updated every 5 years.

Article II

Section 5

A citizen can only lose their citizenship if they have been found guilty of a crime or of disturbing the harmony of the community, and have been declared banished. Arbitration boards have the authority to implement 1, 3, or 5-year jail terms, or banishment. If a citizen is banished they will be taken to a random location and released. If they come back, they will be given a 5-year jail term and then banished again. Note that all decisions by arbitration panels can be appealed twice (refer to Article II).

Article III
Section 1
Currency shall be gold-backed and convertible into gold. Gold and silver coins shall be accepted as legal tender at the current government spot price. Growth in the money supply shall be limited to a maximum of 3% per year, as determined by the main DRB.

Article III
Section 2
Banks, insurance companies, and other finance companies shall all be non-profit. There shall be no stock market, nor any publicly traded companies operating in Isabella.

Article III
Section 3
Business shall use a maximum 25 to 1 pay scale, whereby the top paid employee is paid no more than 25 times the lowest paid. For non-profits, a maximum 10 to 1 pay scale shall be enforced. Any bonus pay or profit sharing will be the same for all employees.

Article III
Section 4
Unions shall be outlawed for both private and public employees. There shall be no collective bargaining. Any injustice or discrimination can be reported to the employment DRB for review.

Article III

Section 5

Inheritance, Gifts, Property, and Real Estate transactions shall be exempt from taxation. The owner of a property shall not be evicted from his property unless an arbitration panel rules in favor of his/her banishment from the community. In the event of banishment, the offender will be paid the current market rate for their property.

Article III

Section 6

A flat tax of 10% on all income will be imposed on all citizens. Businesses will be exempt from income tax. This tax will be due June 1st. It will be paid to a revenue DRB. This DRB will have the authority to assign investigators for irregular tax filings. The main DRB will have the authority to raise this amount in increments of 1%. However, the citizens can overturn this increase (refer to Article I).

Article III

Section 7

A sales tax of 5% will be used for all transactions exchanging goods. There will be exemptions for food, medicine, medical treatment, and real-estate transactions. The main DRB will have the authority to raise this amount in increments of 1%. However, the citizens can overturn this increase (refer to Article I).

Article III

Section 8

There will be a 15% tax on overnight accommodations (for room charges), transportation fuel, tobacco, and alcohol. For consumers who pay this tax, there will be no additional sales tax.

Article III

Section 9

An employee shall work a maximum of 30 hours per week, with overtime illegal. For those who want to work more hours, they can become a government volunteer or start a business. Business owners and volunteers are exempt from this restriction.

Article III

Section 10

The minimum wage will be considered a living wage, and set by the main DRB annually on January 1st. There are two possible minimum wages for both profit and non-profit businesses. The lowest wage is 10 to 1 for non-profit and 25 to 1 for profit businesses — if it is higher than the annual minimum wage.

Article III

Section 11

Both a drivers license and vehicle registration will be free. No physical drivers license is required for driving. However, you must be 18 years old, pass an online written test, and have an adult family member verify that you know how to drive. You can use your Government ID Card for identification. Vehicle registration can be done online, with the registration and license plate mailed to the citizen.

Article III

Section 12

If there is a budget deficit and additional income is necessary, a 10% business tax can be implemented on income over $1 million, with the first $1 million exempt from tax. Also, an import and/or export tax of 10% is permissible if deemed necessary by the DRB.

Article III

Section 13

The only permitted tolls in the County will be on Highway 99, Highway 58, and Interstate 5. It is recommended to only collect a entry toll and not an exit toll. This money will be used to maintain roads and bridges.

Article IV

Section 1

No money shall be given to those in need. Instead, assistance will be given directly to those in need. Public housing centers, public food centers, public healthcare centers, and public job training centers will be supported by the government. Free bus rides to these centers will be available to the public.

Article IV

Section 2

Public housing centers will be separated into different groupings, such as the short-term homeless, long-term homeless, disabled, and veterans. With the availability of public housing, there will be no need for sleeping on the streets and loitering in public places. While some citizens will choose this lifestyle, it will be required for them to live in the public housing centers.

Article IV

Section 3

The public housing centers will be designed to provide a temporary refuge and not a permanent community. It will only provide the bare necessities and not attempt to create a high quality of life or sustainable living arrangement. The food menu will be austere and the amenities just as austere. Conversely, it should provide free counseling and job training. Those residing in these centers should be given help to get back on their feet.

Article IV
Section 4
Any house that has not been lived in for 12 months must be put on the market for sale or sold at auction. Any house on the market for more than 6 months, must be sold at auction. All houses offered at auction, must have an open house for 3 days prior to the auction.

Article IV
Section 5
Single family houses must not be owned for rental income. All Single family rentals must be sold or put up for auction within 6 months of the new constitution. Single family houses will be appraised when the constitution is approved. From that point forward they can only appreciate in value at most 3% per year.

Article IV
Section 6
Multi-unit housing will be allowed as rental properties, although they must be non-profit. All multi-unit housing rental rates will be determined annually by arbitration boards, based on the financial situation of the owner and the current market rates.

Article IV
Section 7
All healthcare related businesses shall be non-profit. This means doctor salaries can be a maximum of 10 times the lowest

salary in the organization. Fees charged to patients will be subject to review by the DRB for potential regulation, and excessive charges can be appealed by patients. Health and nutrition shall be taught in high school for at least a single year. The focus of this education will be on preventing disease and staying healthy.

Article V
Section 1

The postal service, cable service, garbage service, phone service, water service, sewer service, maintenance of roads and bridges will be private and awarded to the lowest bidder every 3 years. The DRB can add services to this list if it is in the interest of the community.

Article V
Section 2

No illegal citizens are allowed to work or reside in Isabella and will be banished if detected. Knowingly hiring an illegal citizen is illegal. All persons living in Isabella prior to the passage of the constitution are eligible to apply for a Government ID Card, which gives them citizenship. A visitor can file for a visa if they plan to stay for longer than 1 year. They can renew this visa if they find work and wish to stay. After 5 years they can request citizenship.

Article V
Section 3

There are no business regulations other than following building codes and honoring the principles of the community. This means polluting the environment will be illegal. A business license is free and can be obtained online. There are no reporting requirements. A citizen in violation of this section can lose their privilege to receive a business license.

Article V

Section 4

All food products sold inside stores must have labels that include the ingredients. No GMO products can be grown or sold in Isabella. No pharmaceutical drugs can be given to healthy animals intended for food production. No herbicides can be used within a city's borders.

Article V

Section 5

No gun laws or drug possession laws shall be created. Except for minors under 21. Industrial hemp farming shall be legal, along with all industrial hemp products.

Article V

Section 6

No fast food chains shall be allowed. No smoking at indoor public places shall be allowed, although private businesses, homes and apartments are exempt.

Article V

Section 7

Any form of advertising to overturn laws is deemed illegal. Any form of advertising that is deemed to be at odds with the community's well-being is deemed illegal.

Article V

Section 8

Natural resource production will be taxed at 75%. Existing publicly traded natural resources companies (oil, natural gas, wind, water) must be sold to private companies within 1 year, or else there will be an auction.

Article V

Section 9

Oil production will be reduced to 75 percent of capacity and then maintained for 10 years. After this period of time, production capacity will be reassessed. The purpose of this reduction is to extend the production life of the wells in order to maintain affordable transportation fuel for Isabella.

Article VI

Section 1

Education shall be the highest priority of the community. Children will get the opportunity for a high quality education. Teachers and principles will be reviewed annually for performance.

Article VI

Section 2

Education will be cost free for students from pre-school through college. However, these will not be public institutions. They will be run by non-profit private companies, with 3-year contracts.

Article VI

Section 3

Students and parents can choose which school to attend. They can switch schools at any time. However, problem students can be relegated to specific schools to ensure high quality education for all.

Article VI

Section 4

Students must pass an exam at the 6th grade and 8th grade level to move forward. They must also pass an exam to graduate from high school to become eligible for secondary education.

Article VI
Section 5
Secondary education will mostly be performed online, with face to face educational settings used out of necessity.

Article VI
Section 6
Police and firefighters will have the option to volunteer after retirement to work part-time until they are 75 years of age. Their maximum weekly hours will be determined by the DRB.

Bill of Rights: Amendments

Amendment 1
Freedom will not be impinged without the guidelines of the constitution taken into consideration.

Amendment 2
Spirituality and religion will be a personal matter and not infringed.

Amendment 3
Freedom of speech and a free press will be protected to the extent that it is not discriminatory or slanderous. No citizen or visitor will be compelled to be a witness or provide information.

Amendment 4
Citizens and visitors will not be imprisoned without a charge. All will have a hearing by an arbitration panel in a timely manner. There shall not be a death penalty.

Amendment 5

No citizen or guest will be subject to unlawful searches or seizures. A person's possessions, be they things, records, or ideas shall not be taken without due process of a arbitration panel. A person's physical and mental health shall be protected.

Amendment 6

Any form of discrimination is deemed illegal. Impacted parties can seek compensation from arbitration panels.

Amendment 7

Whistleblowers who report infractions to the community values will be protected.

Amendment 8

All citizens have the right to file a grievance against another citizen or business. This shall be heard by an arbitration panel in a timely manner. If the grievance is identified as a frivolous complaint, the arbitration panel has the authority to side against the plaintiff.

Amendment 9

Citizens can collect signatures from one-third of the electorate for a referendum to modify the constitution. A two-thirds electorate vote is required to pass the referendum.

Amendment 10

Medical doctors shall require licenses. Holistic healing practices shall be legal and self-regulated. Pharmaceutical drugs shall be regulated. Health supplements shall be regulated but only for the benefit of consumers. The medical community will be largely self-regulating. A Country website to share information about local medical doctors and holistic practices shall be created and open to the public for posting information.

Amendment 11

If the citizens overturn a law, the current DRB cannot create a similar law in the same year. If they do so, a citizen can file a grievance to revoke the law, which will go to an arbitration panel.

Amendment 12

A DRB member can be recalled by an Arbitration panel for unsuitable behavior. A decision in favor of a recall can be appealed twice. If a DRB member is recalled, they will be replaced by an appointment of the remaining members.